Lock and Key

BOOKS BY AARON MARC STEIN:

Lock and Key

Aaron Marc Stein

PUBLISHED FOR THE CRIME CLUB

BY DOUBLEDAY & COMPANY, INC.

GARDEN CITY, NEW YORK 1973

All the characters in this book are fictitious,
and any resemblance to actual persons,
living or dead,
is purely coincidental.

ISBN: 0-385-06732-1
Library of Congress Catalog Card Number: 72-96259
Copyright © 1973 by Aaron Marc Stein
All Rights Reserved
Printed in the United States of America
First Edition

For
Jodie and Len
Smith

Lock and Key

I

For what he had in mind he wanted to be as far away from the building as he could manage, at the least out of Manhattan. He rode the subway to Brooklyn and then he walked, mostly letting himself be led with no regard for where he was being taken. From the people he met along the streets, he'd pick out for himself some woman of decent appearance. The flashy types, the ones who vaunted their attractions, the head turners, the lingering gazers, the hip swingers, the bottom jigglers, all wasted their wiles on him. He wasn't even looking. He was choosing plain-looking women, sensibly dressed, innocent of wiles or of any sort of coquetry.

Choosing one such, he would follow her, moving cautiously at first but steadily bringing his pursuit closer, working up to the move that would make her aware of him and of his intent. Some of them he lost too early in the game, before they'd even indicated that they'd noticed him; but one he followed into a deserted street where there was no sound but her footfalls and his.

Quickening his stride, he began drawing up on her. The sound of their walking was music to him, a percussive excitement built out of the beat of her heels on the pavement and the steadily more urgent rhythms of his own pursuit. She heard it, of course, and when she turned her head to look back, the excitement jumped in him and he had to remind himself that he was not going to break into a run. Steadily and inexorably coming up on her, that was the way to do it.

Then she cast another of those quick, nervous glances back over her shoulder and it was she who broke into the run. That made it different. He ran, too. With every step the distance between them was growing shorter. The thought never entered his mind that he might lose her. Even at this new tempo he kept it as it had been before she ran. He was not gaining on her too fast. A man had to pace himself carefully.

Let the thing speed up and right away it would be out of control, sweeping over you like a great wave that's broken and gone before you even know you're wet. A man had to take his time and pick his time, and then he could get with it and ride its rhythm to build for the full, big, bone-dissolving deal.

He was completely concentrated on himself and on the woman and on the steadily narrowing space between them. The street, as it stretched before them, seemed a limitless track to which the both of them were bound. They would follow this line until there was no more space between them and he could just reach out and have her in his hands.

It had been far out of his thoughts that there would be an intersection or any other place she might turn out to escape from this path which, he felt, was holding them as inexorably as an orbit would. When she did come into the splash of light thrown on the pavement through the broad display windows of a big drugstore, he for the moment had no idea of what it would mean.

When she lurched desperately from her path and threw herself at the drugstore door, he was taken by surprise. He didn't even think that he had better stop running after her. With stupid single-mindedness he ran faster. Only when he himself ran into the splash of light and through the glass of the big windows he saw the woman at the soda fountain, wide-eyed and voluble in a circle of kids, did he have his first thought of danger.

The little girls in the black stockings and the skirts so short they just barely covered their behinds were looking at her with hard and unbelieving eyes; but the boys with the slick, long haircuts and the narrow-legged, tight pants were doubled over with laughter. As he ran into the splash of light, he saw them turn with her pointing finger, and their laughter was turned on him.

He heard no sound of it through the thick plate glass, but even soundlessly its malice and derision buffeted him. He saw the first of the boys make his move, and he saw the way the others began to flow in behind him. He ran on past the drugstore, out of the splash of light, across the intersection. A piece of broken brick zipped past his ear, and behind him he heard those wild hoots learned from TV Westerns and then a great, yapping babble of laughter. It had in it all the malice and derision he'd expected.

He ran as much from their mockery as from them. Aside from whipping him along with their derision, they didn't give chase. He got away. When he had run so far that he heard nothing more behind him, he dropped back to a walk.

He walked until his breathing had returned to normal and his memory of that pack of boys had come down to nothing more than a taste of bitterness at the back of his mouth. He kept trying to swallow it, but his saliva just slid over it and went down. The bitter taste remained.

He chose for himself another woman. This one was a little older, considerably heavier. This one looked as though she would be quicker to try to run, but that any running she would do wouldn't be worth the name. Now, however, he couldn't delude himself that she was tied to any track or that he could set his own pace for closing in on her or that his approach would be inexorable and that she would have no way of escaping him. Now he was only too sharply reminded that she might easily escape him.

They were out in the streets, and even along the most deserted street people can pop out at a man from nowhere. It was not like having her to yourself in a room behind a locked door and the tape slapped tight over her mouth so she can't scream or even cry out. She can make only those little whimpering sounds that go through the nose and reach no ears but his to come at him in the shape of little inflammatory whispers.

There was the unused, leftover urgency from his earlier pursuit, and there was his awareness of the possibility that he mightn't have time to take it as slowly as he would like. This time he came up close behind her and he followed along just the one pace in her rear, close enough so he'd have to do no more than reach out and he'd have her in his hands. When this one would turn off into a deserted street, there would be no waiting before he made his move. All it needed now was that she turn away from these streets that were so crowded with unnecessary people.

When she looked back over her shoulder at him, he grinned into her face. Immediately sensing the intimacy and urgency of the grin, she took fright. Dodging away, she wove back and forth through the street crowd, trying to shake him off; but he dodged and wove with her, and every time she looked back he was right there, grinning into her face. It was as though she were carrying the extra head on her shoulders.

Spotting a police officer, she started plowing straight toward him. As she went, she spoke. She kept her voice low, but she enunciated the words slowly and distinctly.

"I don't know what you want," she said, "but I think you're some kind of a nut and I'm taking no chances. As soon as I get to that policeman, I'm going to tell him to get you off my back. You have until I get to the policeman, so if this is some kind of a gag or something, brother, the fun's over. I'm not looking around. I don't want ever to see you again, and if you're taking off, I don't care which way you go. But if you are taking off, get going, because I mean exactly what I say."

He raised his eyes and looked at the patrolman no more than five steps ahead of them. Their eyes met and it was evident that the officer had been watching him. The patrolman took a step toward them. A bus was taking on passengers at the curb alongside. Without breaking stride, the man reached out and grabbed the rail at the bus door and swung himself to the step. As he came up to the step, he brushed the woman's shoulder. From where he was he could have kicked her. He wanted to, but instead he turned into the bus and fumbled for his fare. He heard the patrolman speak behind him.

"Was there anything wrong, lady?" the policeman was asking. "That man, was he bothering you?"

"What man, officer?"

II

Emily Wilson thought she was the lightest of sleepers.
Any means she could find for shutting away the world
outside she used to help her sleep. What she liked best
about her apartment, therefore, was its quiet. Her bedroom
opened on a back yard so crowded with trees that at least
in summer, when the branches were shaggy with leaf, she
could imagine herself in a house in a forest. These were
not enormous trees. Forest giants don't grow in Manhattan back yards; but still, since the apartment was only one
flight up, there was enough leaf at the level of her bedroom window so that she looked out on a billowing mass
of green. All sight of anything beyond the trees was cut off.

Her neighbors were quiet people. They kept their voices
low. If they had music, it never blared beyond the walls
of their own rooms. They had no raucous parties. Ordinary
city noises coming from outside the building couldn't pen-
etrate to that leafy back yard. Only the occasional fire or
police siren would be audible and even that not shatter-
ingly.

Despite all this silence and peace, however, Emily Wilson required further guarantees of sleep. Every night she
began preparing for bed with a glass of warm milk and a
Seconal. Since she was certain even the faintest glimmer
of light would rouse her, she had a black eye mask, which
made all her sleeping time the deepest night. Since she
was equally certain that even the lightest whisper would

reach down past her Seconal to drag her up out of sleep, she stopped her ears with Flents.

That Friday night in May began no differently from any of her other nights. Methodically she went through the lengthy process of going to bed. Each of her careful preparations she made in turn; and by the time she completed the routine with switching off the light and adjusting her eye mask, she was more than ready for sleep. She was off as soon as her head touched the pillow.

Five hours later she was buried in sleep. Of the little clicks and scrapes of sound that meant the opening of her apartment door she heard nothing. Of the creaking floorboards from which the man, as he crept toward her bedroom, woke those dry, little groans that can sound so loud at night, she heard nothing. Of the man's heavy breathing, as he stood over her, she heard nothing.

The glimmer of light from his small flash never fell on her eyelids. She was wearing her eye mask and even that the light didn't touch. She slept with her arm across her eyes.

Despite all her defenses, however, she did wake. No sleep shop carries for even its most insomniac customer a contrivance to protect her from being wakened by a slap on the mouth. Emily Wilson woke up screaming, but it was a soundless, nightmare scream. It tore at her throat, but all that came of it was some small whimpering which all but died in the passages of her nose.

Her hand darted up to her mouth, but it wasn't even quick enough to touch the tape that held her lips. It had no more than started its movement before it was pinned roughly against the bed. Blind behind her eye mask and deaf inside her Flents, Emily Wilson surged past the Seconal to a full consciousness of the man's weight when it came down on her.

Hopelessly she fought him, but she was never a match

for his heavy strength or for the brutal power of his animal drive. Then he was finished, and she had given up fighting him.

"It's over now," she was telling herself. "He's done it to me. He's had what he came for. It's over. I must be very still. I must wait for him to go away. Later, after he's gone, I'll have to begin thinking of what I'm to do now; but till then I can't think of anything but being completely quiet and waiting for him to go away."

It never entered her thoughts that she might try to snatch off her eye mask and see the man. Somehow not seeing him made it a little more bearable. In her mind there was even some confusion between not seeing and not being seen.

Before she ever came out of that confusion, it was too late. With the same speed and the same accurately aimed violence that slapped the tape on her lips, his hands came back to her. With all of his weight behind them, he rammed her throat. If she struggled then, it was only an automatic flailing of limbs. Quickly and efficiently the man's hands squeezed her back to sleep and past it to a stillness that needed no defenses against waking.

When the man left her, Emily Wilson was dead. He was gone only a few minutes, and when he returned he had with him a brace and a bit, a chisel and a screw driver. He also had with him a shiny new lock, complete with two shiny, new keys. Working neatly and carefully, he bored the hole in her apartment door and chiseled out the corresponding slot in the door frame. Carefully and neatly he installed the lock, tested it, and cleaned up after himself. Re-entering the apartment, he found Emily Wilson's purse and into the purse he dropped the two new keys.

"Better late than never, baby," he whispered.

Leaving the apartment, he let both the locks snap to behind him—the one he'd opened when he first came to the apartment and the new one he had just installed.

III

Saturday morning the corner news dealer sold one paper less. The supermarket around on the avenue checked out for delivery one grocery order less. Neither noticed the loss. One less New Yorker stood in line for a Saturday night movie, but who would notice that?

Her neighbors across the hall were away for the weekend; but since they never had any interest in her comings or goings, they wouldn't have missed her in any event. It was not until Sunday afternoon that Emily Wilson was first missed, and even then it was hardly more than somebody noticing her absence. Nobody was worrying about her. It was her Philharmonic Sunday, a day in her season's series of subscription concerts, and for the first time in all her years as a subscriber her seat was empty. Hers was one of the low-cost subscriptions. In her part of the concert hall people took their music seriously and concerts were never lightly missed. Under no circumstances were concert tickets wasted. So, when her seat was empty throughout the concert, her neighbors did notice. It irked them. They called it inexcusable. You can always find someone to use a concert ticket. You can always sell it or give it to a friend. A crime to waste it.

Emily Wilson had been twenty years in the one office, and in all that time she'd never missed a day. She'd never even been tardy. At nine, when she wasn't at her desk, it caused comment. At nine-fifteen it caused concern, at nine-thirty alarm. If it had been anyone else, somebody would have gone around during lunch hour to see what might be wrong. Since it was Emily Wilson, there could be no doubt that something was seriously wrong. Only a disaster could be keeping her away, and it would have to be something more than a disaster that was keeping her from telephoning.

At ten a brisk and efficient young man from her office was at the apartment leaning on her doorbell. At 10:05 he was in the basement of the building shouting for the superintendent, a man named Les Gilman who knew Miss Wilson to be a lady who liked to keep herself to herself, and Les Gilman didn't know whether Miss Wilson was going to like it at all if they went into her apartment.

"All you've got to do is open the door for me," the brisk young man told him. "I'll take all the responsibility."

"There's doors can be opened," Les said stubbornly, "and there's doors that can't be opened."

"I know. You're afraid she won't like it. Let me worry about that."

"Look, mister," Les chuckled, "that ain't all I'm letting you worry about. You can also worry about how you can open a door when you ain't got no key."

Brisk young men who spend their lives in offices have little patience with slow-thinking people who work with their hands and who don't use their heads. With the deliberate and carefully enunciated argument that brisk young men fall into when they are holding exasperation painfully in check, he tried to reason with Les.

"My good man," he said, "you're the super here. Certainly you have keys to all the apartments, or you have a master key."

"Sure I got keys, but not to that new lock she just put on her door."

"Suppose there's a leak in there or a fire and you have to get in?"

"That's what I want to know, mister. Suppose there's

a fire and I can't get in. The whole building, it can burn down while I'm waiting for the firemen to come and break down the door."

"You're sure she didn't give you the key to her second lock. People usually do. Isn't it a law or something?"

Les shrugged. "I don't know about no law," he said. "But it's in her lease. It's in all their leases. No extra locks on their doors without they give me the key."

"Then how come she didn't give you a key?"

"I ain't seen her since she had that lock put on. I ain't seen her the whole weekend. Saturday morning I'm cleaning the halls and I see the lock. I ring her bell so I can remind her how it is in the lease and she'll give me a key. She wasn't in then, and she ain't been in since whenever I tried. Look, mister. She's gone away. You know, a weekend."

"The weekend's over. This is Monday."

"So it's a long weekend."

The brisk young man went back over the whole thing again. He was from Miss Wilson's office. Miss Wilson, who'd never been a minute late, much less absent, didn't come to her office. She hadn't phoned to say she wasn't coming. She just hadn't appeared.

"She's an old woman," the brisk young man said. Any woman in her fifties would be twice his age, and from where he stood she looked old. "She's had a coronary maybe or a stroke or one of those things. She's lying behind that door in a coma. She needs help."

The super shrugged it off. "She picked a bad time to be needing help," he said unfeelingly, "right after she's put the extra lock on and not given me no key to it."

"What about a ladder?"

"What about it?"

"With a ladder I could get in by a window."

Les was having no part of that. It wasn't his job helping

anybody to go into apartments through windows. A young
fellow comes along and says he's from Miss Wilson's
office. How does Les know he's even what he says he is?
Les never saw this young fellow before. Les isn't giving
him any ladders to go in any windows.

The brisk young man wasn't too impatient with Les's
stubbornness. When a young man is interested in getting
ahead, he needs unusual and difficult situations. Without
them how will he ever demonstrate his resourcefulness or
his executive ability?

Bristling with both, the young man went out to the
street and found a policeman—Patrolman Frank Giordano,
shield number 954376. Patrolman Giordano was also
young. He was also bent on getting ahead. He went back
to the house with the young man from Miss Wilson's
office. He heard what the young man had to say. He heard
what Les had to say. He looked at the lock. He tried his
finger on the doorbell. He remembered a case two blocks
over where an old woman who lived alone fell in her apartment and lay two days with a broken hip while she
scratched at the wall for help. For two days that old
woman's neighbors complained about mice in the walls.
Patrolman Giordano decided it was time to act. He asked
Les for a ladder. Confronted with the uniform and the
shield, Les couldn't ask how he was to know whether
Patrolman Giordano was who he said he was. Les provided
the ladder. He carried it out to the yard and he set it up
under Miss Wilson's bedroom window. Giordano climbed
it and went in the window.

After that police routine took over. Precinct detectives
swarmed through the building. The men from the police
lab examined the door and its locks. They examined the
windows and the tree that stood just outside the bedroom window. They dusted for fingerprints. Homicide
checked its files for rape killings. The Vice Squad did a

file check for rapists and sexual deviates. The Medical
Examiner's office did the post mortem. A nephew, Miss
Wilson's only living relative and heir to her life savings,
saw her for the first time in ten years when he came east
from Michigan and claimed the body to take it home for
burial. The brisk young man took care of the office col-
lection. Miss Wilson had flowers for her funeral.

In most quarters she wasn't long remembered. The brisk
young man wired the flowers and put the whole thing out
of his mind. In three days the newspapers had the story
wrung dry and went on to fresher sensations. After that
very few people remembered it at all unless they happened
to be apartment hunting and seeing the place reminded
them; but there were a few. Patrolman Giordano remembered. He couldn't easily forget his first sight of her. The
precinct detectives remembered because for them she was
unfinished business and nothing irks a precinct detective
more than unfinished business that shows no promise of
ever converting into finished business.

The building had no fire escapes. There was the back
yard tree with the branches that came right up to the bedroom window, but they had checked the tree. Its trunk
was strong enough to take a man's weight, but it was a
New York tree with branches hardly thicker than a man's
thumb. Under the weight of even a small boy the branch
that reached out to tap against the glass of the dead woman's window would drag down to where it would be far
below the level of the window.

There wasn't as much as the smallest scratch on either
the door or the lock.

The detectives listed all the possibilities that presented
themselves to them: a ladder, keys to both locks, a key to
the new lock and a celluloid strip for the standard job that
was on all the apartments in the building, a human fly, a
man she knew so well that she had let him in.

For making up this list they had the assistance of the Police Department's homicide specialists. They also kicked it around with the men from the Vice Squad.

"She's wearing a mask over her eyes and plugs in her ears and she lets a man in?" Homicide asked.

"Nothing but the mask and the ear plugs to indicate that she didn't," Vice Squad said.

"Seconal. She'd taken Seconal. A dame doesn't do that unless she's planning on sleeping alone."

"But a man turns up and she changes her plans," Vice Squad persisted. "She's got the eye mask handy. She's got the ear plugs handy. She's taken the Seconal. He turns up. She lets him in. Things go out of control. He kills her. Not so good for him. This isn't a kid with a hundred boy friends. We start asking is there a man who could come at night and she'd let him in. Someone will know about him. How does he go about making it look different?"

"He beats the door up a little and he puts some scratches on it," Homicide suggested. "He fixes it to look like this was a man who had to break in."

"No," Vice Squad said. "That's hard to do without being noisy. Why take risks when he's got right to hand an easier way and one that's completely quiet? Slip the eye mask on her. Shove the plugs into her ears. That changes the picture. It's no longer the man she could have let in. It's a man who sneaked up on her."

The precinct detectives ran down all the available lines. They looked for a man whom Emily Wilson had known so well that she would admit him to her apartment even after she was all ready for bed. They found nobody. No one had ever seen or heard of such a man. If they drew a blank in this direction, equally they drew a blank on their other line. They never did find the locksmith or the hardware store that sold Emily Wilson that new lock for her door.

IV

Along with Patrolman Giordano and the precinct detectives there was another man who remembered Emily Wilson. It was Les Gilman. He could hardly forget her if only because to him fell the job of showing prospective tenants the apartment where she died. Through the window of his basement quarters he watched them come. There were women singly and women in pairs. They carried the New York *Times* folded to the apartments-to-let-three-four-five-rooms page.

Many of these women came only as far as the pavement in front of the house. They looked at the front door. They looked up at the windows. They shuddered and went away. Others, the older ones perhaps or the brawnier, came and looked at the apartment, but there was about them an attitude of wariness and an aura of excitement which indicated that they were just looking, punctuating the boredom of the serious search with a morbid inspection of these premises where a woman could live so dangerously.

They asked questions and Les, soberly and carefully, answered everything they asked. He recited the rental, the landlord's readiness to paint, the possibility that a new refrigerator might be subject to negotiation. None of them asked about the heart of the matter, and Les, of course, didn't bring it up; but uniformly they left saying that for one irrelevant reason or another it wouldn't do or at best that they would have to think it over. Les knew they would think about it, but never in terms of taking the place.

It was all sight-seers the first day, and they did keep him reminded of the dead woman. On the second day he had a real prospect, a pair of young men. They were impressively heavy-jawed, heavy-fisted, and heavy-shouldered. They looked the place over and they thought it would suit them fine.

"What are you asking for it?" they asked.

Les added a fictional fifty dollars a month to the rent Miss Wilson had been paying. The two prospects whistled.

"For what?" they asked.

"For the apartment."

"This apartment?"

"I ain't showing no other apartment."

"It's not worth the half of that."

Les shrugged. "Look," he said. "I don't set the price. They tell me what they're asking for it. I say what they tell me."

"It's not going to be easy to rent."

"It's been vacant before," Les said. "Never been no trouble renting it, a nice, quiet apartment like this."

"The nice, quiet apartment in which this old babe's been raped and strangled."

Les grinned at them. "Either of you worrying something like that'll happen to you?" he asked.

"That makes no difference, what we're worried about. You have that happening in a place, it brings the rent down."

"Not here it don't," Les said.

"The place needs painting."

"Only if you don't like the color," Les said. "It's good paint, washable. You can wash it down."

"They're not painting?"

"They painted last year," Les said. "It ain't due for two years more."

"They've got a nerve."

"Look," Les told them. "Nobody's holding no gun to your head. Nobody's making you take it."

"You're damn right. We're not. In fact, you can take it and shove it."

"You don't want to pay what it costs, you don't want to pay it," Les said. "That's all right. You don't have to get mad."

They went away and Les went back to his basement window.

So the memory of Emily Wilson stuck in Les Gilman's mind all of that week. He had the vacant apartment and he had the people who came to look at it. They kept him reminded. Then Claire Burns turned up. Claire was a change from the others. She was so spectacularly cheerful. She was also spectacularly outspoken.

She stood on Les's doorstep and, steadying herself against the door frame, she looked him over. Under her arm she had the *Times* folded to the right page. Hanging from her lip she had a cigarette. Her eyes were startlingly blue and the smoke didn't bother them at all. Les was tempted to ask her whether she had come to look at him or at the apartment. He waited for her to say something, and while he was waiting she finished looking him over. It was evident she'd decided she didn't care much for what she saw, but she said nothing.

After several moments of this Les was feeling awkward. "Want to see the apartment?" he asked.

She ran a hand through her froth of flame-colored hair. "Not particularly," she said.

"Then what can I do for you, ma'am?"

"Nothing. Not a solitary thing. I'm taking the dump."

"The apartment? Without even looking at it?"

"What's to look at? It's the place nobody wants. I'm the tenant nobody wants. We go together, the apartment and me."

"It's a nice apartment," Les said. "Nice and quiet."

She laughed. "Maybe it won't be once I'm in it," she said. "Okay, friend. Show it to me. We might as well go through the motions."

They went through the motions.

"It is nice," she said. "You want a deposit or the first month's rent?"

"Deposit, and you fill out the application. The office will let you know."

She nodded. "You go through all the motions," she said. "Even here. The office will check my references. 'We very much regret that we cannot recommend Mrs. Burns. The lady is an alcoholic.' You know what that means, friend? The lady is a lush. In case you haven't noticed, the lady is right now what most people would call stoned. This, friend, the way I am now, is sober for me. I have to be sober. I'm looking for a place to lay my head."

"Mrs. Burns," Les laughed, "are you alone or are you going to be a couple here?"

"I'm never alone when I can help it, but if it's Mr. Burns you're asking about, he's back home in Texas with the third Mrs. Burns. I was the second. The first gets nice alimony and I get nicer. You see, with her it wasn't so much that he stopped wanting her as it was that he started wanting me. With me it was different. He started wanting Number Three but, more than that, he was sick and tired of my drinking. It's worth a lot to Mr. Burns to have me off his hands. In case the office cares, friend, financially they couldn't want for a better tenant."

When they checked, the office found it exactly as the lady represented it. All her former landlords were agreed. The lady was financially reliable. She was always admirably prompt in the payment of her rent, but that was the only respect in which any of them found her at all reliable. Otherwise, if there was any sin a tenant could commit, Claire Burns had committed it. Her cigarettes started fires. The tubs she ran while she was having that other little drink caused floods. Her parties were drunken and raucous. When she wasn't giving parties, she was going to them and after those she didn't always make it all the way back to her apartment. When she slept on the stairs, neighbors tripped over her.

Ordinarily the office would have reached for any other prospect, but ordinarily there would have been other prospects. This, however, was special. No other woman would consider the place at any price and oddly, so far as the office could know from Les's reports, there had been only women coming around to look at it. Les had further reported that the women were coming around only out of curiosity. So there was this financially reliable Mrs. Burns, always prompt in payment of her rent, not asking for any reduction, not asking for anything at all. Too bad that she was so prone to cause damage, but on the other hand she did have a good record for being amiable about paying for such damage as she caused. What did they have to lose? If necessary, she could always be dispossessed.

So Claire Burns moved in. If the first time Les had seen her the lady had been stoned, on moving day she was smashed. She arrived riding in the moving van. She seemed to be on the most amiable terms with the moving men, possibly even on intimate terms. As soon as they had unloaded a sofa from the body of the van, she came falling out of the cab.

A young man, loitering on the sidewalk, sprang forward and caught her. This was a ponderously built, ordinarily slow-moving, and always slow-thinking young man, but he had quick reflexes. When only quick action could save her from falling, he moved with speed and easy grace; but once he had her and was holding her upright, he stood clumsily supporting her in the circle of his heavy arms; and, obviously unable to imagine what he was to do next, he did nothing.

"Don't just stand there," Claire said. "Take me to the sofa."

"Maybe you want to go inside," the young man suggested.

"There's nothing inside," Claire told him. "I don't want to go in there until the furniture's in. Take me to the sofa."

The sofa was standing on the sidewalk. Claire needed much help. The young man all but carried her to it. Relaxing in a corner of it, she patted the place beside her.

"Sit down," she said. "I can't go on looking up at you. It makes me dizzy."

Laughing, the young man sat beside her. "I could use a drink," he said.

"Who can't?" She waved vaguely in the direction of the van. "It's in there," she said. "Bottles and bottles, but they say they can't get to it till they unload what's on top of it. Crazy putting stuff on top of it, isn't it?"

"Real crazy, lady."

Claire grinned at him. "You're ugly," she said. "You're the ugliest kid I was ever on a sofa with, but I like your muscles. What's your name?"

"Bob. What's yours?"

"Claire. Bob what?"

"Bob Herman. Claire what?"

"Claire Burns. Stick around. When they get the stuff moved in, we'll have that drink. We'll have a whole flock of drinks. It's the only way to get started in a new place, with a party."

"You moving in here, Claire?"

"No. The boys are moving in. I just drive the van."

"You're kidding."

Claire studied him for a long moment. "You don't just have muscles," she said. "You're smart, too. You saw right through me. I can't fool you, Bob. I am kidding."

"What do you want to go moving in here for, Claire?"

"A girl's got to live somewhere. Why not?"

"A dame was living here . . ."

"And she got herself raped and killed. That won't happen to me."

"It can happen to anybody."

"To you, Bob?"

"I mean anybody, she's a dame."

"Not anybody. No gal can get raped unless she's unwilling. Me, I'm willing."

The moving men were ready to take the sofa upstairs. Claire told them to take it.

"Not with you people on it, Mrs. Burns."

"Why not?"

"We move furniture. We don't move poeple."

"Union rule, I bet," she growled. "That's what's lousing everything up, the lousy, interfering unions."

Bob Herman got up off the sofa. "Leave her there," he suggested. "We can carry it in with her on it. I'll help you."

"We don't need no help from you, bub, and we don't carry nothing in with nobody on it. She rolls off of it and hurts herself. It's us as gets sued."

Bob shrugged and turned back to the sofa. He took Claire's hand and tugged. "Come on, Claire," he coaxed. "You got to get up, Claire."

Claire didn't move. She was either asleep or pretending to be. Bob bent over her. Sliding his big arms under her, he lifted her off the sofa. Smiling faintly, she let her cloud of red hair settle against his shoulder. One of her shoes fell off and one of the men picked it up and tossed it on the sofa. They picked the sofa up and carried it into the building. Bob followed with Claire cradled in his arms.

Upstairs he put her on the sofa again. Standing over her, he scratched his head. Then slowly and clumsily he straightened her into a more comfortable-looking position. He put the shoe back on her foot. He pulled her skirt down and smoothed it. After that he stood for a while with his heavy, broad-palmed hand curved around her thigh. It was the way it had been when she had first come tumbling down from the cab of the moving van and he caught her and held her; but now there was a difference. Claire wasn't telling him what he was to do next.

The moving men came and went, bringing stuff up into the apartment. Coming past Bob with a heavy chest of drawers, they jostled him. Those ready reflexes took over. His hands darted upward. They closed into fists and even while he was turning, they were in position, bobbing in front of his chin where he had it tucked down tight to his chest—the left fist slightly in advance of the right. He was ready, but he was without an adversary. The men, staggering slightly under the weight of the chest, were moving away from him. Shadowboxing as he went, he danced lightly around the room. You could find boxers who moved better than Bob Herman did, but it was only when he was moving this way that he moved well at all. This gave him a formula to follow. It gave him the feeling he only rarely had otherwise. It was the feeling that he knew what he was doing.

The chest had been the last of the furniture. Now they were bringing up cartons and packing cases. Bob stopped in front of a likely looking carton. It was tightly corded with the rough red-and-white twine the packers used. He patted at his pockets, trying to remember whether he had a knife. He had none. Squatting beside the carton, he worked his blunt-ended fingers under the twine and tried to snap it between his hands. The cord bit into his flesh but he disregarded that. He was ready to fight it till his hands bled and to go on fighting it with bleeding hands. Bob Herman could take it, and if there was ever to be any alternative to taking it, it would never of itself come out of Bob Herman's head. Someone would have to suggest it to him.

The suggestion came but in the wrong way. Les Gilman through his basement window had watched their meeting in the street. He had seen Bob carry Claire upstairs. Following along, Les had been hanging about in the hall outside the apartment's open door and he'd been watching. Now he came in behind Bob where Bob squatted at the corded carton. Les moved silently. For Les it was a habit to move silently.

Standing over Bob, he watched him strain at the twine.

"Okay," he said softly. "What do you think you're doing?"

Bob didn't turn from the carton. "Got a knife on you?" he asked.

Les decided it was time to turn him. Taking a small, carefully studied practice swing with his foot, he planted the toe of his workshoe with neat precision in Bob's left buttock.

Bob surged up from the floor, bringing his punch with him. The moving men watched but they didn't interfere. Bob backed the super into a corner. Fingering his bleeding mouth, Les turned to the moving men.

"Get this guy off of me," he mumbled.

The moving men weren't taking a hand.

"What's the beef?" one of them asked.

"This guy comes in from nowhere and he starts fooling around with her stuff," Les told them.

"I was going to get the unpacking started for her," Bob explained.

"We packed it, and we unpack it," the moving men told him. "Any damage, we're responsible. Somebody else touches it, we ain't responsible."

"Okay," Bob shrugged. "Where'd you pack the liquor? She wants that unpacked first."

"She don't care what's unpacked first," Les growled. "Anything gets stolen, who's responsible?"

It was a question Bob didn't like. His left fist went wrist-deep into Les's belly. His right cut Les's cheek. Les's back banged hard against the wall and he slithered down it. He sat on the floor with Bob hovering over him. The men moved then. They pulled Bob off. Les waited till they had Bob well away from him.

"All right," he said. "Somebody go get a cop."

The moving men ignored him. They talked to Bob instead.

"Look, buddy," they said, "why don't you go home? We got our work to do. She's paying by the hour. She's paying for packing and moving. She ain't paying for breaking up fights."

"She asked me up for a drink," Bob said stubbornly. "I got as much right here as anybody. I got more right here than he has."

"Somebody get a cop," Les repeated. "Then we'll see who's got a right here."

"We got our work to do," the moving men told him. "You want a cop, you go call one yourself."

Les scrambled to his feet. "Okay," he said. "Okay. I'll get a cop myself. You hold the bastard here."

"We got our work to do. We ain't holding nobody."

The two who had been holding Bob let go and stepped away from him. Bob took one step toward Les and the super scuttled to the apartment door. Bob didn't follow.

"Go get your cop," he jeered. "I'll be here. I ain't going nowhere. She asked me up for a drink."

Nursing the cuts on his mouth and cheek, Les ran down the stairs. The elder of the two moving men tried to give Bob a bit of advice.

"He's not just talking, kid," he said. "He'll be back with a cop. What do you want to hang around for? You don't need no trouble."

"I don't need no shithead kicking me in the ass. That's what I don't need."

"You got all the best of it. You knocked him on his. You opened up his lip for him and you opened up his cheek for him. What more do you want?"

"She asked me up for a drink. I'm staying here and I'm having that drink."

"Look at her. You think she's going to be in any shape to give anybody a drink?"

"That's another reason for me staying," Bob said stubbornly. "You know where this is?"

"It's West Twelfth Street. That's where it is."

"It's the apartment where the last woman she lived here, she got herself raped and murdered. That's where it is. Look at her. She in any shape to take care of herself?"

The moving man shrugged. "Friend," he said, "most people we move we see them the once and then never again. Her we see all the time. This is the fifth time we've moved her. Five times in less than two years and every time, before we've got everything in and everything unpacked, she's just like this. Still she always comes out all right."

"Never before in this place here," Bob insisted.

He stayed. The movers went back to their work, leaving him hulking in the middle of the room. After a few moments he was itching with self-consciousness, trying to think of something he might do that would make him look more as though he belonged there. If Claire hadn't passed out, they could have been sitting on the sofa to-

gether, having drinks or not having drinks. The drinks
weren't important. On the sofa with Claire either way
he could be looking right.

Or if the moving men were letting him help them, he
could have been feeling right. He had the strength for lifting stuff and for moving stuff around, and there he was
just standing there while the men kept walking around
him at their work.

In his thoughts he began rehearsing what he would do
and say if or when Les came back with a policeman, and
standing as he was out in the middle of the room, he could
think of nothing that didn't sound too impossible and too
foolish. The one thought that did keep coming back at him
was how easy and natural this could be if Claire weren't
passed out.

He lumbered over to the sofa and stood over her, wish-
fully looking for some sign that she was coming out of it.
She was giving no sign. He reached down and touched
her. Feeling his hand on her arm, she did stir but that was
all. Cupping his hand part of the way toward making a fist,
he cuffed her lightly at the side of the chin. It wasn't anything, just the gentlest brush of his knuckles.

Her lips parted in a slackly vague smile and her breath
blew a small bubble out between them. The bubble burst
as her lips closed back again. Taking her by the knees, Bob
gently moved her legs deeper into the sofa, making room so
he could perch on the edge of it. He sat and there was just
barely enough room for him. He could feel the shape of her
ankles where he had them pressed against his hip. He was
on the sofa with her, but he was still feeling as awkwardly
wrong and as foolish as he'd felt standing out in the middle
of the room.

More for want of something he could do with his hands
than out of any clear intent, he began stroking her legs.
Moving up to her knees, his hand paused there a moment

and then slipped under her skirt. He was past the top of her stocking, but he was barely aware of touching the skin of her thigh. With an oddly prudish neatness, he used his free hand to pull her skirt down and straighten it where his exploring hand had rolled it back a bit.

Abruptly he was feeling natural and at ease. All the troublesome awkwardness was gone. Never given to questioning himself, he had no thought of questioning this. This was one of Bob Herman's things, always feeling most at ease with himself when his hands were out of sight. It was the same as when they taped his hands. As each layer went on, he would feel more relaxed and easy. Then when the big gloves went over the whole thing, he would feel completely his own man. But a kid can't live his whole day in gloves, and all of the rest of the time Bob's hands were looking for a place to go and hide themselves.

There had been a time when it was a lot easier. Kids like Bob Herman spent most of their waking hours with their hands in their pockets. They never had any need to think about it. It was what pockets were for. Automatically a man's hands buried themselves there. That, however, was before pants came so tight. Bob grew up in jeans and chinos and, when they fit a man like another skin, he can't just slip his hands into his pockets and lose them there. He has to force them in, and even then they aren't out of sight. They are merely covered the way the first layer of tape covers them. Through the tight-stretched cotton every knuckle shows up clearly molded, each finger, every nail.

By the time Les Gilman came back with the policeman, Bob was comfortably at ease. His self-consciousness was forgotten. He felt as though he belonged, as though nobody could question his being where he was. That the policeman should have been Patrolman Frank Giordano, shield number 954376, gave it a pleasant little plus value. With Patrolman Giordano Bob was completely at ease.

"Frankie," he chuckled. "I'm a dangerous guy, Frankie. You better put the arm on me, Frankie."

A flicker of annoyance crossed Patrolman Giordano's serious young face. He did his best to pretend that Bob hadn't spoken. Turning to Les, the patrolman was crisp and official.

"This the man?" he asked.

"Look at him," Les howled. "Just look at him, what he's doing. Like they was alone maybe. You blame me I want you should get him to hell out of here?"

"You coming along to bring charges?" Giordano asked.

Les pointed indignantly at his face. The blood had stopped, but a noticeable puffiness was developing.

"Look at me," he said. "Look what he done to me."

"Yeah, sure. You charging him with assault?"

"You're wasting your time, Frankie," Bob said amiably. "He's charging nobody with nothing. Next time he'll look twice who he's kicking in the ass."

"You kick this man?" Giordano asked.

"I got to get him out of here. Something happens to her, who'll be responsible?"

"Not what I asked you," Giordano said patiently. "I asked did you kick him."

"Who's marked? Him or me? Who's got rights here? Him or me? Why don't you ask him what he's done, or is he maybe a buddy of yours?"

"I asked did you kick him?" Giordano repeated less patiently.

The moving men came back into it. "He come up behind this guy and he kicked him. It wasn't no accident or like that. He got himself set, he took aim, and he let him have it. The guy came up swinging. The guy slugged him. We wasn't here to break it up, the guy would've knocked the damn head off of him and, just between us, Officer, we didn't want to break it up except they could get blood on some of her stuff or maybe bust something, and right now, till we get it all unpacked and we're out of here, if anything gets damaged, it's us has to pay for it."

Patrolman Giordano turned to Bob. "Okay, kid," he said. "What brings you here?"

Bob grinned. "Ain't you heard, Frankie?" he chuckled. "This is the place where dames get raped. Me, I'm a rapist."

Patrolman Giordano hadn't forgotten Emily Wilson. He scowled. "Not funny, Mr. Herman," he said sternly. "Knock it off. Knock it off right now."

"Okay, then. She brung me here. She asked me up for a drink."

"You meet her in a bar?"

Before Bob could answer, the super put his word in.

"On the street. On the sidewalk right here out front. I seen the whole thing."

It was nothing more or less than Bob himself had been preparing to say, but now that the words had come out of Les, he felt that he couldn't use them any more.

"Is it anybody's business where I met her?" he blustered. "I met her. That's all. She said I should come up for a drink. That's all. She didn't say there was anybody else had any rights here, and she didn't say they was anybody she'd given a license to give people a hard time. She said I should come up for a drink. That's all."

"And she's passed out," Giordano added, "and giving no sign she's going to come out of it enough to give you any drink."

"I can wait," Bob said stubbornly.

"Wait?" Giordano argued. "What for? You don't need a belt that much. Anyhow you're better off not drinking. It's bad for your wind. It puts fat on your gut."

Les was finding this whole exchange most unsatisfactory. If his opinion had been asked, he would have told you that this Patrolman Giordano was no kind of a cop at all. For all the good he was he could just as well not have been carrying a billy or a .38. There wasn't even anything to tell you he had any hands. The way the cop was dealing with Bob Herman, he could have had no more than a mouth to him.

"Look, Bob," Giordano was saying. "I'll walk you around to the gym. Take yourself a workout with the heavy bag. You'll do yourself more good that way."

One of the moving men found humorous connotations in the reference to the heavy bag. Laughing, he explained the joke to the other.

"The kid had ought to give hisself a workout with the heavy bag," he said. "He can't do himself no good with this one."

Giordano didn't like it any better than Bob Herman's joke. His face reddened, but he let it pass while he went on trying to persuade Bob.

"You can come back and see her another time," he suggested.

"Nobody wants him around here," Les put in. "Not now, not never."

Bob started his move, but he carried it only far enough to send Les sidling behind Giordano.

"Okay," he told the patrolman. "I'll walk along with you now, but, if Bigmouth is smart, he'll always keep himself a cop handy because he's never going to know when I'll be taking a notion to come back."

Giordano started for the door. "If you're walking along," he said, "then walk. What do you want to go making yourself trouble for?"

"It won't be my trouble, Frankie," Bob promised him. "It'll never be my trouble."

V

Nobody could say Les Gilman didn't try. He waited for the first time he could catch the new tenant sober, and that wasn't an easy thing to do. A man had to be watchful and patient and he had to keep after it. Then, when his chance did come, he had to move fast. For Claire Burns sobriety was never more than the most temporary state. Whenever she found herself in that unhappy condition, she moved promptly and decisively to rectify matters.

On his first attempt he began too late. The lady already had a couple of drinks in her and, since all the time he talked to her, her attention was divided between him and the bottle, and the division steadily slanted more toward the bottle than toward Les's arguments, her sobriety didn't last nearly long enough for him to begin making his point.

He tried again and eventually his timing was good enough to catch her while she was still trying to locate a bottle out of which she might have her first drink.

"That lock on your door, Mrs. Burns," he began.

"What about it?"

"I was thinking how maybe you'd want me to get the cylinder changed for you. You know, a new cylinder, different keys."

"What for?"

"Somebody you don't know, he's got a key to it the way it is. You'll want it fixed so nobody gets in without you knowing him."

"Why?"

"You don't want just anybody walking in here any time."

"Don't I? Why not?"

"Because it ain't safe, Mrs. Burns."

"Locks are safe?"

"I get the cylinder changed for you. You have new keys. That's safe."

"Even if I never lock it?"

"But you got to lock it."

"Why? Give me—let's see—twenty-five good reasons."

"It's dangerous without having your door locked. Anybody can come walking in."

"Nobody's come walking in yet."

"There's always a first time, Mrs. Burns."

"Not for me, there isn't."

"You're no different from anybody else. You leave your door unlocked and people will be walking in."

"God, my good man, takes care of fools and drunkards. I'm no fool. I stay drunk all the time."

It had the sound of logical argument and the shape. Les found it unanswerable, but he couldn't allow himself to be bested this way. Logic was one thing and safety another. Les Gilman was concerned with safety.

Instead of arguing, he tried coaxing. In the course of even this brief exchange, Claire Burns had found time to down a couple of formidable drinks. Les didn't have forever.

"Look, lady," he said. "You just let me get that cylinder changed for you. Will you, huh? Not for nothing but just for a favor to me. Yes? How about it?"

"One drink leads to another," Claire said, pouring her third, "and one favor leads to another as well. I let you change the whatsis, not for anything but just as a favor to you. It won't stop there. You'll be giving me new keys and as another favor to you you'll be asking me to take care of them and not lose them. And then it'll be something more, more favors to you. I'll have the lock with the new doohinkus and I'll have the keys and I'll be taking care of them and not losing them, and then you'll be wanting me to lock the door all the time and unlock it and lock it up again and all that jazz."

Overcome with the prospect of this labor and monotony Les was intent on inflicting upon her, she had an overwhelming need for a fourth drink. She made it a good one and after that it was as it had been before. Moment by moment Les could see her slipping away from him. He was losing her to the bottle again.

It wasn't that she didn't go on discussing it with him. It was rather that she switched back to logic and there was no appeal Les could make that would move her out of her relentlessly logical position.

A lock to which some unknown rapist and murderer held a key was no better than no lock at all. Any woman who bothered to lock her door when it had such a lock on it was either a fool or else so peculiarly particular that she wanted to be raped and strangled by nobody other than this one unknown who held the key to the lock.

"Since I am no fool and I am not peculiarly particular," she explained, "I leave that lock alone, and all I ask of it is that it leave me alone. I don't lock it. I don't touch it. I ignore it."

"That's what I mean," Les persisted. "You let me get the cylinder changed. You let me get you new keys. You have like a new lock. You have a lock there's some point in locking. Nobody you don't want in gets in."

"If I lock it and if I don't lose the keys. I've never bothered to lock doors. I've never worried myself hanging on to keys. I'm not starting now. So what'll I have? An unlocked lock. You tell me what makes one unlocked lock better than another unlocked lock and I'll listen. So now go away and think up an answer to that one. Don't just stand there. You slow me up on my drinking."

Les went away, but he wasn't ready to drop the matter. He just bided his time till he could again catch her in a sober moment. He couldn't manage it often, but he was watchful and he never did let an opportunity slip by him. Since he was never able to think up a fresh argument or a novel approach and she never troubled to think about the matter at all, each of their discussions of the lock followed the same pattern; and, after they had been through it a few times, the mold had hardened to the place where they were even repeating the same words.

As the days passed, it became obvious to Les that he wasn't alone in his preoccupation with setting up some protection for Claire Burns. He had an ally in this endeavor; but since this ally was Bob Herman, the alliance brought Les Gilman no pleasure. He would have preferred to be alone.

Bob Herman came around regularly. Hardly a day passed without his spending some part of it in the apartment. Some days he drank with her. Other times he didn't drink at all. Which he did would depend on how he happened to find her. He never appeared early enough in the day to come on her before she had started down her well-worn road toward oblivion.

Taking up with her wherever she was, Bob rode along with her. He never drank with her drink for drink. Up to a point she would refill both glasses as soon as they'd been emptied, and when she was past that point she would have him take over the task of keeping the glasses filled. Whichever was doing the refilling, however, his pace was so much slower than hers that she took two or three refills to each one of his.

There was no calculation in it. Theirs was a live-and-let-live, drink-and-let-drink relationship. To each according to his thirst. She hardly ever went out and she had no guests other than Bob. All she required in the way of company he was providing. She required little. There were those days when he found her in a state so little removed from sobriety that, drinking along with her even at his far more moderate pace, he would, by the time she was passed out, be so far down the same road himself that he would lie down beside her and together they would sleep it off.

Just as his drinking rate was far slower than hers, his recovery rate was the more rapid. When he wakened, he would steal quietly away and always he was most careful to see that the door to the apartment was securely locked after him.

More often he would come on her when she was already well on the way. On those days she would pass out while he was still quite sober or at the most only mildly buzzed. Any of these times he could have stayed on drinking alone, but he never did. He would leave her to sleep and, as he went out of the apartment, he was always careful that the door should be locked after him.

Once or twice he turned up after she had already finished the familiar journey. Then he would just look at her and see that she was all right and he would quietly take himself off, again taking great care to lock the door which, every time he came, he found again unlocked.

Les Gilman was aware of Bob's every coming and going, but on one occasion when Bob Herman had been there it was specifically called to Les's attention and to that of everyone else in the building. That one time Bob dropped around and found Claire out, but differently this time. She wasn't in the apartment, passed out behind her unlocked door. She had gone out to a bar. For a change she was doing her drinking elsewhere.

Bob came in as usual. Whenever he dropped around, he was punctilious about announcing himself. Even when the door stood ajar, he remained outside it and rang the door-bell, waiting till she would sing out her invitation to come in. Only when after several rings he heard no invitation, did he venture to enter uninvited, and those would be the times he would find her passed out. This one time he went in expecting that it would be more of the same and he found that she wasn't there. He left as he had all those other times, locking the door after him.

Later when Claire came home it was exactly as she had always told Les it would be. The door was locked and she didn't have the key. She stood at her door bawling for Les to come and open up for her and loudly berating both Les and Bob for their silly ideas about keys and locks.

The night the man came to her, she lay in a drunken sleep behind her locked door. Her defenses against waking were every bit as good as Emily Wilson's had been. The key slipped into the lock and she didn't hear it. The door swung stealthily open and she neither heard the sound nor felt the draft that came slicing through her rooms from the outer hall. As he came across the floor toward her, she heard nothing.

Just as it had been with her predecessor, it was the slap of the tape seal across her mouth that roused her, but she wasn't roused so far that she was trying to scream. She may have mumbled some sodden and sleepy protest, but even without the tape across her lips it would have been faint and feeble at best.

Then when the weight of the man came down on her, there was again a straining of the tape to indicate that she was making some sort of a sound walled up behind it. That one might have been a giggle. There was no knowing. The man showed no interest in finding out. He could have been some electronic automaton programmed for stealthy entry, rape, murder, and the cleanup afterward, and he would hardly have been more clickingly inexorable in running through the full sequence of his program.

He lifted himself off her. He stood over her. He rammed his hands against her throat, tightened them, and squeezed. When he lifted his hands away, Claire Burns was dead. He left the apartment, but again he wasn't gone long.

Again he returned with tools and a new lock. Working carefully and quietly he removed the lock that had never been locked on Claire Burns except by Bob and quietly and carefully he replaced it with the new lock. Since the new one was identical in make and model with the old, the change was quickly made without boring any fresh holes in the door. When he had finished there was little cleaning up to do; but what there was to do he did with the greatest care. He had in his pocket a soft rag. With it he rubbed to a high polish everything he had handled.

The old lock he left in the apartment, carefully stowing it on the upper shelf of a kitchen cupboard. With it he left the key that fitted it even though he had to ransack the apartment to find it. He looked virtually everywhere before he turned it up in a drawer otherwise given over to jugs of face cream and boxes of powder. It was greasy with the cream and coated with the powder. The man took it up with a pair of small pliers and handled it only with the pliers. Claire Burns had been no more careful of her key than she had claimed to be, but the man was most careful.

That left him with the two keys that belonged to the new lock. One of these he deposited in the drawer with the creams and the powder. The other he put in the pocket of a gray leather jacket that lay thrown across a chair in the living room. Satisfied that he'd done everything that needed doing, he left the apartment, pausing only to make certain that the new lock had sprung to behind him.

VI

The next day, following his custom, Bob Herman dropped around. He found the locked door. So far as he could determine it was exactly as he left it when he staggered out of the place the day before. Always previously, though, during his absence Claire would have been at it and the door would again be unlocked.

He rang repeatedly and had no answer, so he went off. There had been a few times when she did go out and all too often he had arrived to find her in a state where nothing possibly could rouse her. He was, therefore, completely unconcerned. Being a youth of uncomplicated mind, he found it easy to believe that people could change and it pleased him to think his example and exhortations had finally been fruitful.

"The babe's learned sense," he thought. "She's caught on to what locks are for."

He tried her again later in the day and again he was unsuccessful. The following day he went around early, choosing a time when he had every reason to expect she would answer his ring. It was too early for her to have gone out and even too early for her to have more than just barely started on the day's drinking, if at that early hour she would have started at all. It was so early, in fact, that he expected she might still be sleeping off the effects of the previous day's dosage, but a time when the sleeping off process should have been far enough along for there to be no difficulty at all about rousing her.

When even at that hour he had no response to his ring, he began for the first time in his life to experience mixed feelings. There was pleasure in the thought that she'd learned to lock her door and there was some pride in the belief that she had the lesson from him. On the other hand, there was a growing irritation with that same locked door. It was fine that she was now locking it, but it was annoying that, in effect, the door was locked against him.

He kept on trying and, by the time another day had passed, he was back to what for him was a more customary state of mind, one simple attitude and one uncomplicated emotion. Over the wide range of hours he'd been trying her she couldn't have been drunk beyond rousing all the time. Also if at all such hours of day and night she was out of the apartment, it had to be that she'd gone away.

He kept telling himself it was all right with him, but it wasn't. He resented her going away without telling him, and it angered him that she should go off that way with never a thought to the possibility that he might at some time before she returned want the jacket he'd left in her apartment.

The more he thought about it, the more he was angry. Going off and leaving his jacket locked in her apartment, it just went to show. All the time and trouble he'd been taking over that crazy stewed tomato and her not even stopping to think maybe he'd need his jacket. So the hell with her. He was through worrying about her. He wanted no part of her any more. All he wanted now was his jacket. It was a good jacket, maybe not exactly new, but as good as new. It still had plenty of wear left in it and, even if it didn't, he liked that jacket.

Now that he was thinking about it, it was a lucky jacket. The first time he wore it, the very day he bought it, was the day Jake got hit by the cab and was laid up with the broken arm so he couldn't fight Colzano. It was only Jake's

broken arm that got Bob his shot at Colzano. Without
that Bob would still have been waiting, and a fighter goes
no place waiting. It was only the Colzano knockout that
got anybody noticing him at all. That had really been the
beginning for him, the Colzano bout.

Before that you said Bob Herman and people would only
ask, "Who he?" Now people heard the name, they said,
"Yeah, the kid knocked Colzano out." That knockout began everything for him, and the way a kid has to figure
his luck, it was the jacket that began everything for him.

He wasn't long thinking about it before the jacket had
become all important and Claire Burns was of no impor-
tance at all. He was no longer merely impatient to have his
jacket back. The recovery of that jacket had become the
mainspring of his life. He had himself convinced that unless he had it back, his luck would go with it. He'd had
some bad days when he'd worn the jacket, but Bob was a
cheerful lad with no memory of his bad days. Everything
he associated with the jacket was good.

He began to think that even in the couple of days he
had been locked away from his jacket his luck had been
turning. They'd been gloomy and disagreeable days and
Bob attributed their mood to being without the jacket.
It never entered his mind that he was missing Claire. She'd
been cheerful company. Her silly good humor suited him
perfectly. Without her, life was dull and lacking in laughs.

But Bob was preoccupied with the jacket. He had to
have it back and quickly before his luck turned completely
sour. If it had been anywhere but that apartment of
Claire's, he could have managed it easily. He could have
gone around to the house and explained about the jacket,
and the janitor or somebody would have the key. The janitor could get the door open for Bob and Bob would get his
jacket.

There'd be no trouble about proving it was his. Everybody knew Bob's jacket. He hardly ever wore anything else. Everyone in the neighborhood knew it and all the studs over at the gym.

If it hadn't been in Claire's place where the very first day he had that go-around with the jerkoff super . . . Anybody else in the neighborhood, anybody else in the world, Bob would go to the man, show him how the deal stood, ask him the little favor.

But Gilman—Bob wasn't going to that shithead, not for anything, not even if he never had a lucky day in his life again. There wasn't anything wrong with asking favors. You could ask favors from anybody, particularly such a little, easy favor, but here you've got a jerky squirt you hated on sight and you never got to like him any better on knowing him more.

So asking Gilman was out, even if it wasn't obvious that anything Bob asked of him would be refused if only for the pleasure of saying no. With Les Gilman, Bob would have to be devious and Bob didn't know how to begin.

What did start him was running into Frank Giordano. Ordinarily running into Giordano would have seemed nothing special. Frankie was a patrolman. He was attached to the local precinct. He was the neighborhood cop on the beat. He wasn't any fighter, but he did come around to the gym sometimes to work out. He was all right, was Frankie. He liked the fight game and he liked fighters. All the studs around the gym knew Frankie and Frankie knew them all. Frankie was a good guy, and you can't say that for all the cops.

Bob had reached the place where he wasn't going into the building to ring Claire's doorbell any more. He'd had enough of that. Even that came to seem like asking a favor and asking it in the wrong quarter. Bob had learned to hate the sound of the bell as he heard it through that locked door. In his ears it had a pleading sound like the crying of some kid wanting to get in somewhere he wasn't wanted. Bob was angry. He didn't want to ask anyone to let him in. He was in the mood for something more manly, something like a direct assault on the place.

When he ran into Giordano, therefore, he'd already taken to patrolling the street outside Claire's place, glaring at the building, even hoping that Les Gilman might come and try to give him a hard time. He was enjoying the thought of what he might do to Gilman, what he should have done to the crumb back at the beginning. He wasn't thinking that what he had in mind would bring him no closer to his jacket.

The jacket was a practical problem and, trying to cope with it, Bob was having a cheerless time. What he could do to Les Gilman was a daydream, and thinking about creaming the man gave Bob pleasure. A man has to have some enjoyment in life.

From way down the street Giordano saw him. He saw the challenge in Bob's walk and in the set of Bob's shoulders. He could read Bob's mood and, piecing the mood together with that particular stretch of street, Patrolman Giordano, who was a good man and a good cop, immediately smelled trouble. So Frankie Giordano came up on Bob, and there was nothing casual about Frankie but his manner.

"Hiyah, Wonderboy," he said.

Bob almost grinned at him. These were friendly words and Bob always had a ready response to friendliness. This time, though, the grin was stillborn, because the name took him right back to the Colzano fight. He scored the knockout. They called him Wonderboy. He had the jacket. Without the jacket the word was a mockery.

"Hiyah," Bob growled.

"You wouldn't maybe be looking for trouble?" Giordano asked, but still keeping it light and casual.

"I wouldn't be looking to run away from none."

They were walking along together and they'd come to the place where Bob would have to choose between continuing on with Giordano or doubling back to pass the house again. He turned back and Giordano stopped him.

"The word's around you've been making time with her," he said.

"Who's passing the word?"

"It's just around."

"And you believe everything you hear?"

"I believe a kid, when he's gone as far as you have, he needs to be a little smart."

"And what's a little smart?"

"Staying away from dames, staying away from all dames."

"You see me with a dame?"

"Staying away from all dames," Giordano repeated, "and particularly from dames they're older than you. They've had time to learn things you haven't even heard about yet, and most particularly from dames they're lushing all the time and they get you to where you're tying one on, too, all the time and nobody's got to tell you what that'll do to your wind."

"Nobody's got to tell me," Bob growled

He turned away and started back to pass the house again. Giordano turned with him and walked by his side.

"You and her," he said. "You've had a bust-up. So what? It's the best thing could happen to you."

"You been hearing that, too? That we had a bust-up, her and me?"

"Maybe I can read the signs."

"Maybe you better go back to school. You don't read good."

"Then what's eating on you, kid?"

"Ain't nothing eating on me."

"You don't act it."

"Look, this dame, she's nothing to me. She never was nothing to me. Don't let anybody tell you no different."

"You're wearing the sidewalk out in front of her house for nothing?"

"Since when is it your job saving the sidewalk from wearing out?"

"Never mind what's my job," Giordano said. "I'm talking to you like a friend."

"So I'm worried about her. Any law been passed makes it no good I should worry about her?"

"What's to worry? She run out of gin?"

"A couple of days now I ain't seen her."

"Hooray for you. You've got to learn when you're lucky, kid."

"Look," Bob said. "I only been trying to keep an eye on her, taking care of her like. You know what place it is she moved into, and she only just learned she should lock her door."

"And when she wasn't locking her door, you weren't worried about her?"

"I was. That's what kept me coming around, but . . ."

"But what?"

"But I don't know. She's got her door locked and she don't answer the bell and that old babe used to live there, it happened to her only after she had the extra lock put on her door. I don't know. Ain't you ever been worried just because you was worried without you're able to give reasons or like that?"

Bob wasn't really thinking it. He was thinking only that his lucky jacket was locked inside the apartment and Claire had gone away. He was thinking there had been the previous time when that same door had been locked and a man had suggested to Giordano that something might be wrong in there and it had been enough to make Giordano go in. Why wouldn't Giordano do it again? All Bob had to do

was worry Giordano enough and Giordano would go in
there. Bob could go in with him and there would be his
jacket and not a thing in the world wrong and there'd be
no trouble about his taking the jacket out of there, not
after the number of times Frankie had seen him wearing
that same jacket and the number of times Frankie had
dropped by the gym and they'd gone out of the gym together, Bob lifting the jacket off the hook on the way out
and sometimes Frankie even lifting it off for him. Frankie
knew that jacket so well that, even when there were a lot
of jackets lined up on the hooks, he'd pick out Bob's jacket,
just from knowing it, and hand it to Bob.

"How long she been locking her door?" Frankie asked.

"Only the last couple, three days, only since last time I
saw her."

"Before that, didn't she have a lock?"

"Sure, she had a lock, the lock that was on there when
she moved in. I kept locking it for her and she never locked
it at all for herself."

"And now it's locked without you locking it for her?"

"That's right. Like I told you."

Giordano was trying to make some sense of it. He knew
what Bob didn't know, that a search had been made for
the locksmith who sold the lock and installed it on that
door. He knew that no such locksmith had ever been
found. If it was still the same lock, then presumably there
was a man who had a key to that door, the man who once
used his key to come in on Emily Wilson and who could
have used it again to come in on Claire Burns. There could
be such a man, Giordano was thinking. There almost certainly was such a man, but why would he wait through all
the time when Claire Burns was leaving her door unlocked
and anyone could have come in on her? Why would he
wait till the time when only he could do it?

It made no sense; but Patrolman Giordano was a good

man, and he could never make sense of anything a rapist-murderer might do. It couldn't hurt if he had a look.

"You're thinking maybe he came back?" he muttered. "The one who did it to that other woman?"

It was working. Bob would be going in with Giordano. It just needed one more small push.

"There was this guy," Bob said. "You ain't never caught up with him."

Giordano was only a patrolman. He had yet to make detective. If there was any taunt in Bob's words, Frankie could easily have passed it off as not directed at him. Giordano, however, was too much a cop to think that way. This sounded like criticism of the department, and at that moment Giordano felt he was the department.

"It couldn't just be," he asked, "that you've split up, you and her? It couldn't just be you're looking for a way that maybe I'll get you back in?"

"Look," Bob growled, "did I ask you for anything?"

"All right, all right. We'll check up on her."

They went to the house and upstairs Patrolman Giordano tried the doorbell. Under the pressure of his finger it seemed to have a different sound. This wasn't any kid crying to be let in. This was peremptory. It had authority behind it. Even heard only faintly through the locked door, it had the sound of authority in it. It wasn't any please-let-me-in sound. It was a this-is-the-police-open-up sound.

The door, however, remained locked and nothing came from behind it but the shrilling of the bell. Giordano didn't wait. He went to Les Gilman.

"This Mrs. Burns you've got upstairs. When did you last see her?"

Les yawned. "Her?" he said. "I don't rightly know. You got a houseful of people and you see them coming and going all the time, you don't keep no track which one you seen and which you ain't seen."

"Seen her in the last couple of days?"

"Not so I remember."

"She's got her door locked and she don't answer the bell," Bob contributed. "A couple days now it's been like that."

Les said nothing. He was waiting to hear something further from Giordano. This was a meeting of minds between two men of authority. Contributions and comment put in by outsiders or hangers-on were to be brushed away. They were like the buzzing of flies.

"That lock on her door?" Giordano asked. "That's been changed since the last tenant?"

"Which lock you talking about, the regular one goes with the door or the extra one?"

"Either of them," Giordano told him. "Both of them."

With the leisured deliberation of a thinking man asked a question in an area where he's publicly recognized as having authoritative knowledge, Les gave Patrolman Giordano the benefit of his learning and acumen.

"On them doors," he said, "we got the regular locks. They're like a part of the door. They go with the rental, and for them we're kind of responsible. Then there's extra locks. A tenant puts one of them on, it's the tenant's lock and the tenant's responsibility. Except the tenant's got to give me a key to any lock she puts on, those extra locks they ain't no business of mine."

"Yeah, sure," Giordano interrupted. "Except everybody knows about those regular locks. They're not good for anything. All it takes is a knife with a thin blade or a strip of celluloid and anybody he wants to can slip them back. He don't have to be a pick-and-loid man. Anybody can do it."

If Giordano felt he stood for the police authority as a whole, Les Gilman was standing for the property owners.

"They're all the locks you're going to find on most of

the apartment doors in the city," he said. "People want different locks, they put them on."

"Sure, sure," Giordano said. "Mrs. Burns, did she have a new lock put on?"

"No."

"Did she have the cylinder changed in the old one?"

"No."

"She have the cylinder changed in the regular lock?"

"You said yourself nobody even needs a key to open one of them regular locks."

"That's not what I asked. I'm asking did she have anything changed."

"No. That Mrs. Burns she keeps the whole works unlocked. She don't care what kind of riffraff comes in. Why would she go changing locks or cylinders when she don't never carry keys or know where she put them, and she don't never lock any doors?"

"She's had the door locked the last couple of days."

Les shrugged. "Not that I know about," he said. "If anybody locks her door up there, I'm usually the first to know about it. She comes to me to open it up for her. She never knows where she has her keys."

"You have keys?"

"I got keys to all the apartments. It's in the leases. They can't go putting no extra locks on without they give me the keys."

"Okay," Giordano ordered. "Get your keys. We're going in there for a look."

"Sure," Les said. "I'll get them."

Les went back into his apartment for the keys. They waited at the door for him.

"It's in the leases they got to let him have keys," Bob growled. "If I lived here and if I had one of them outside crappers, I wouldn't give that jerk even the keys to that, lease or no lease."

If Les heard him, he was giving no sign of it. Within a few moments, he was back with a pair of keys, both neatly tagged. Carrying them as though they were his badge of authority, he led the patrolman and Bob back upstairs to the door of the apartment. There he tried the door and satisfied himself that it was indeed locked. This was his domain and in his domain he was taking nobody's word for anything. He tried the doorbell.

"We've been ringing," Giordano told him. "There's no answer."

Les ignored him. He applied his finger to the bell and rang again. He addressed himself to the task with the manner of a man who stood alone in the world in his special expertise in the ringing of doorbells. Eventually he indicated that he was satisfied that even to his ring there would be no answer. Only then did he bring the keys into play, but his handling of them also was given that special touch of the professional insider. The key to the ordinary lock he inserted in its keyhole. The key to the extra lock he inserted in its. When both were well seated in their respective keyholes, he tried to work them both simultaneously, one with each hand. The lower key turned easily. The key to the extra lock wouldn't turn at all.

Scowling, Les withdrew it from the keyhole. Carefully he studied the tag he had tied to it. It was marked with the right apartment number. He compared it with the tag to the key to the other lock. The apartment number was the same on both. This was a thorough man, Les Gilman. He was checking and counterchecking.

Returning the key to the keyhole, he tried again. Nothing happened.

"It should work," he muttered.

"Let me try," Giordano said.

Without yielding his place in front of the door, Les scratched his head. "It should work," he repeated.

Giordano shouldered him out of the way and grasped the key. It wouldn't turn for him any more than it would for Les. He withdrew it from the keyhole and put it back in again most carefully. He tried driving it in hard to seat it well. He tried drawing it back a little, seeking out some delicate matter of alignment. He jiggled it. He tried coaxing it and he tried forcing it. Nothing happened. He checked the tag, and despite the number on it, he asked his question.

"You're sure it's the key to this apartment?" he asked.

"That's what the tag says. I go by the tags."

"He goes by the tags," Bob jeered, "and shithead gets them tagged wrong."

"I go by the tags," Les repeated, still ignoring the buzzing of flies, "and I ain't changed no tags since the last time she asked me to get my key and open up for her because some son-of-a-bitch's been and locked up on her."

"And it worked then?" Giordano asked.

"Of course, it worked then. It worked like the other one's still working. I let her in, didn't I?"

"With this key?"

"Sure, with this key. You seen the tag."

Giordano sent him back downstairs to bring up all his keys. Protesting that keys to other locks wouldn't work when the key to this lock wouldn't, Les went. He was making it clear that he had no faith in it, but he was going along. This was an unfathomable situation. He was a man confronted with the impossible, and in an impossible situation can a man do better than trying the impossible, even though reason tottered at the prospect?

While he was gone Bob and Giordano took turns at wrestling with the recalcitrant lock.

"You know what shithead's gone and done?" Bob suggested. "He's got the key to some old lock that was once on this door and he's given us that one instead of the one that belongs."

Giordano shook his head. He was examining the tags on the two keys. The one on the key that worked in its lock was fainter in its marking. The ink on it was older and it had faded considerably. Also the tag itself was worn and limp. The tag on the key that didn't work was crisp and new and the ink on it was clear and fresh.

"Key or no key," he sighed. "We're going to have to get in there, kid."

Bob backed off a bit. "Give me room," he said. "I can crash the door with my shoulder."

Giordano held him back. "We'll wait and see if he comes up with another key."

Les came up with a whole box of keys. All of them were neatly tagged and he went through the lot, taking each in turn without any regard for what it said on the tag. Nothing worked.

"You know what's happened," he said. "The lock's jammed. It happens sometimes. Something slips inside them and they won't work. You've got to get a locksmith to put them right."

It was a word Giordano had been trying to keep out of his thinking. A locksmith could have changed the cylinder in the lock or he could have replaced the old lock with a new one. Same brand of lock, same model, they look so much alike nobody can tell one from another.

A woman has a locksmith in and he keeps a key for himself. It happened once. It can happen again, even if lightning doesn't strike in the same place twice and Frank Giordano remembered that from school. It was a crock. Some places are just like that. They draw lightning. In places like that lightning strikes all the time, not just twice, all the time.

"We can get in there quicker than that," he said. "Remember that ladder you found for me the last time?"

VII

This time around nobody bothered to look for locksmiths. This one was too open-and-shut for that. Even from the very first, even before any of the detectives or the police specialists were in on the act, it was open and shut.

There are those cases in which the police can be suspected of snatching at the first and most convenient suspect and settling for him, but this one was never such a case. If Bob Herman was the first and most convenient suspect, at the first he was also the suspect nobody wanted.

Patrolman Giordano was a good man, a good cop, and a good friend. Giordano, as he went up the ladder to the bedroom window, was mumbling to himself.

"Frankie," he said. "You're in a rut, Frankie."

Then he climbed in the window and it was all so much the same that only gradually he began to take notice of the differences. There was the woman's body on the bed. There were the changes that come to a body with death by strangulation. There were the further changes that occur during the first few days after death has taken possession. There was the tape securing the lips and the peculiarly blank expression it gave the face. It seemed to underline further the expected blankness of death.

Where on Emily Wilson it had been a sensible night-gown, torn and crumpled to leave her lying naked in its wreckage, this time it was a frilly, chiffon thing such as Giordano had never seen until his wedding night and not again since. Mrs. Giordano that one night wore a thing

like that over her nightgown and he even remembered
what she called it, nothing as everyday as a dressing gown.
She called it a peignoir.

So Claire Burns had gone to her bed with this peignoir
thing on her and nothing under it, and now in death she
lay naked in the wreckage of it. There was that small difference; and thinking about it, Giordano came to notice
a couple of other small differences. Unlike the Wilson
woman, Claire was wearing no eye mask. Unlike the Wilson woman, her ears were not stoppered with the little
Flents.

Giordano, adding up these trifling differences, was ap-
palled by the disproportionate enormity of their sum. This
one wasn't the mixture exactly as before. This one lacked
just those very details which in the Wilson case produced
the police concentration on locksmiths.

Even in the Wilson case, there'd been the thought that
the eye mask and the Flents and the sleeping pill were
not necessarily conclusive evidence of a killer the victim
had not voluntarily admitted to her apartment. Giordano
knew that even on that one there had been a police search
for a boy friend. He also knew the search had been fruitless.
Now he had this other babe and there wasn't the first
thing about this one to suggest to anyone that they look
for anything but a boy friend.

Giordano winced away from the thought. Just on the
other side of the locked door to this woman's apartment
his friend, Bob Herman, was waiting.

"Wonderboy Herman," Giordano muttered, trying to
pretend he wasn't feeling kicked in the gut and reminding
himself that he was a cop and that the day he put on the
uniform he'd given up forever this privilege other men
had. Frank Giordano had his job to do. He had no right
to feel kicked in the gut.

Bob was a good kid and a not bad fighter. Bob had it

in him to go places. This was a kid with a future and Frank
Giordano had been worrying about this kid. It wasn't as
though Frank had been noticing nothing or as though
he hadn't sensed that Wonderboy Herman could have
been headed for trouble. Hadn't he just a little before
been telling Bob that taking up with this Claire Burns bag
was maybe something that could do a kid no good?

Headed for trouble? Sure. But there's trouble and
trouble, and what was there ever to say a kid could be
headed for this? Patrolman Giordano never had the first
moment's doubt about what he had to do. He didn't have
to like it, but he had to do it. Also he wasn't kidding himself any about the way the thing looked, but he could tell
himself that more often than not things weren't at all the
way they looked.

So Bob was in trouble. Ever since the day the kid first
met this Burns twist, he'd been around her all the time.
Even before anybody started looking, Wonderboy was
going to be the first candidate; but wouldn't that be only
before they started looking? A bag like her, all gin and joy,
look at the way she got started with Bob. If it was that
easy, it had to be that it wasn't only Bob.

Anyway you looked at it, Giordano thought, Bob Herman was the kid who was right in there. He was the one
who had it made and, when a kid's got it made, what need
has he to do a thing like this? It would have to be some
other boy friend, another pickup as easy as Bob. When it's
that easy getting started, a man's naturally going to be
expecting something, and there would be this other guy
who wasn't getting any. The way Bob was around all the
time, how much could there be left over for another stud
to get?

Giordano's mind never ran to fancy phrases like "wish-
ful thinking," but still he had the idea of it hanging in his
head as he went to unlock the apartment door. He was

wondering whether he had any really good reason for thinking it couldn't have been Bob Herman, some reason better than his just wanting it not to be Bob.

He opened the door. Les had put the ladder away and he was back in the hall waiting with Bob. The two men came into the apartment. Les stopped just inside the door. Bob darted a quick glance around the living room, trying to remember where he had left the lucky jacket. He remembered tossing it down somewhere in the living room. Within the moment he spotted it where it lay across the chair.

He sauntered over to it and was about to pick it up. Giordano had been totally unaware of it until he saw Bob reach for it. His reaction was immediate.

"Leave it, kid," he barked. "Don't touch anything. Don't neither of you touch anything."

Startled, Bob backed away from the jacket. Then on a quick second thought he turned to Giordano and protested.

"I ain't touching nothing it ain't mine," he said. "It's my jacket."

"I said leave it."

"You seen me wearing it. You seen it on me plenty of times. You know it's mine."

"I know it's yours," Giordano said grimly, "but leave it. Don't touch it."

"Look, Frankie," Bob bleated. "What the hell's come over you?"

"Never mind what's come over me. When were you up here last?"

"Yesterday. All day yesterday I kept coming up here and ringing her bell. I left the jacket here. I kept coming around, trying to get my jacket back."

"Not then. When were you here last and she was here?"

Counting it back aloud, Bob worked around to the day.

"Yesterday," he counted, "the day before. It was the day before that."

"Tuesday?"

"Yeah. Tuesday."

"Tuesday night?"

"That's right. Tuesday night."

"Late?"

"What difference does it make? Late? Early? I don't know. It was night."

"And that's when you left your jacket here?"

"Sure. That's when."

"Tuesday night and you don't know what time."

"Look, man. We was here. We was drinking. She passed out. Right here on the floor here she passed out. I picked her up off of the floor and I carried her inside and I put her on the bed. I wasn't passed out, but I wasn't sober neither. That's how come I went off and left my jacket. A guy's so stoned he don't even know he's leaving his jacket, he's so stoned he ain't knowing what time it is either. What difference . . ."

He was only going to repeat his earlier question, but Les broke in on him before he finished.

"Three forty-five in the A.M.," Les said. "That was when he went out of here. Three forty-five in the A.M. Wednesday morning. All the way down in my apartment I heard him. He come running down the stairs and he was falling down more than he was running even. He was making so much noise, he woke me up. I looked out to see who it was and I seen him. I seen him come out of the building. I thought that noise, that time of the night, all the neighbors would be complaining. I looked at the clock to see what time it was. Three forty-five in the A.M."

Bob scowled. "It was a lot earlier than that," he said.

"How much earlier?" Giordano asked.

"A lot earlier," Bob repeated.

"He said it himself. He wasn't noticing the time," Les growled. "I was the one got woke up. I was noticing the time."

"You say earlier," Giordano insisted, ignoring Les. "How do you know?"

"It was only half past nine, maybe ten, I come up here. We wasn't here drinking that much time. We couldn't have been."

"But you don't remember?"

"I remember enough. It wasn't all that long a time."

Giordano shook his head dolefully. "You don't remember nearly enough, kid," he said, and then he turned to Les. "You," he said, "when did you see her last?"

"Tuesday evening. She came in after dinner Tuesday evening."

"Alone?"

"Alone."

"What time?"

"I wasn't taking any special notice of the time. After dinner. Eight o'clock maybe, maybe later."

"Did you see this man come in?"

"No. I only seen him leave. I seen him leave twice."

"Twice that night? Tuesday night?"

"Yeah. If you call Wednesday in the A.M. Tuesday night."

"You've already told me about that, three forty-five A.M. Wednesday morning. That was once. What about the other time?"

"A little after eleven. I was putting the trash cans out before I turned in for the night. I saw him come down while I was putting the trash out."

"That's different. That would be about the time," Bob said.

"But he came back later," Les insisted.

"All right," Giordano said. "Don't touch anything either of you."

"What's wrong?" Bob asked nervously. "She inside? She in there? Something wrong with her?"

"Shut up, kid, and don't go touching anything," Giordano told him.

"Something's happened to her," Bob said. "I'm going in there."

"Sorry, kid," Giordano murmured. "You're not going anywhere."

"I'm her friend. I got the right."

"Sorry, kid."

Giordano picked up the phone and called his precinct. Cupping his hands around the telephone mouthpiece, he spoke into it as softly as he could. Both of the men were obviously straining to hear, but they remained where they'd been standing, not venturing to come in closer.

Keeping it curtly and correctly official, Giordano was quickly through on the telephone. He'd made his report and there was nothing more for him to say, but he did wish there could have been some way for him to prolong it. The telephone, for those few minutes he was busy at it, was a barrier between him and Bob Herman. The minute he hung it up, he would be again caught in the conflict between what the good man would have liked to do and what the good cop had to do.

Bob waited only until the phone was back in its cradle. "She's dead," he said. "I want to see her."

The precinct detectives were on the way and Giordano knew they'd want Bob to look at the body. They'd be taking him in and making him look at it, but they wouldn't take it kindly if it wasn't left to them to give him his first look. Frank Giordano was no detective. He was just a patrolman. It was his job to report in and to keep things in hand until the precinct detectives arrived and took over.

"It's time you were thinking of yourself, kid," Frankie said gruffly.

"Like what? Like I take my jacket and walk out of here like she wasn't my friend and like I never gave a damn what happened to her?"

"Like trying to remember Tuesday night, everything you can bring back, important or not. You can't remember too much before you'll have to start answering questions about it."

"That's crazy. I remember. I remember we was drinking and she passed right out here on the floor. I remember I picked her up and I carried her inside and I put her on the bed. I remember I went out of here and I fixed the door so it locked after me. I remember I tried it and made sure it was locked." He jerked a thumb toward Les. "He said I come back later. He says he heard me on the stairs and he looked out and seen me going out downstairs. Me, I don't remember none of that. Maybe I come back and maybe I didn't. If I come back, I didn't get in because the way I left her she was too passed out to be getting up and opening any door for anybody and, without she got up and let me in, I couldn't get in because I locked the door myself before and I tried it so I was sure it was locked. How could I get back in without I had a key?"

"And you had no key?" Giordano asked.

"How would I have a key? She never had one herself. I kept locking her door for her because it was crazy the way she was always leaving it open so anybody could come in here. Every time I locked it on her and she was out, she had to get him to let her in with his key. She never had hers." He looked toward Les. "He'll tell you."

They both were looking to Les, waiting for him to speak. He took the time to choose his words carefully.

"She never had her key," he said, speaking with the studied deliberation of a man who is eager to testify only to what he absolutely knows and to nothing more than that. "Whether she was always mislaying it or losing it or giving it away to people I don't know. All I know is she didn't never have it. She came home and the door was locked, I always had to let her in."

"And your key always worked?" Giordano asked.

"Of course, my key always worked. Any time my key didn't work she'd know it and she'd have to have the lock fixed. I'd have reported it to the landlord and he'd have made her have it fixed. You can't have no apartments where nobody can get in where there's a fire or something like that."

"And all of a sudden when we have to get in, your key isn't working."

"All of a sudden," Les said, "all of a sudden somebody comes here and the door's locked and he has no key and he messes around with the lock so that somehow he gets in, but messing around with it that way, he's wrecked the lock and now the key won't work in it any more."

Giordano examined the lock. "This don't look like anybody's messed with it," he said. "No scratches, no marks, no nothing. It looks like a brand new lock."

Les smiled indulgently. With the lofty manner of the expert who condescends to let some ignorant layman into the secrets of his science, he explained away Giordano's objection.

"What's messed up in that lock," he said, "is inside. You can put scratches all over the outside of it. You can knock dents in it. You can let the outside get all rusty, but it will work just as good. It's what's inside a lock that counts, not the part you can see."

It was all to do again with the detectives. When they first arrived, they told Giordano to keep Bob and Les where they were till the detectives would be ready to talk

to the two men. They went on into the bedroom. Giordano
and his two charges waited.

Then the detectives came out and it began. They
questioned Les Gilman and they questioned Bob. Gilman
told his story exactly as he'd told it to Giordano except
that for the detectives there was more of it. After all,
Giordano had been there himself the day Claire Burns
moved in. There had been no need to tell him anything
of how Bob Herman had come to be what Gilman called
her "steady."

Mantled in a manner that bespoke a man wholeheart-
edly dedicated to the truth, the whole truth, and nothing
but the truth, Les gave them his whole package.

"Every time I seen them," he said, "he had his hands
on her. The first time they met I seen it. He had his hands
on her before he even ever spoke to her."

Then again: "She was a heavy drinker, was Mrs. Burns.
They was always drinking together till he got her passed
out. Of course, I never seen them how they were together
then except the first time. It was that first day and she
was moving in here and the movers they was all the time
up and down with the furniture and stuff and the door
standing open with them going in and out all the time.
He had her in here then and her passed out on the sofa.
I seen them that time, him on the sofa with her and his
hands up under her skirt."

That was the big difference between Les and Bob. Les
remembered everything and with the most admirable ac-
curacy. Bob remembered little, and even what he did remember he was always fumbling around in his mind.

Bob had never been a thinker, and the effort they were
demanding of him, that he try to think and try to remember, made him truculent. At the beginning they had
nothing to go on but the data they'd had from Les Gilman,
and that gave Bob a focus for his truculence. There was

all the stuff Les remembered that Bob couldn't recall at
all, and then there was also the stuff of which he did have
some recollection, but never quite the way Les remembered it.

He didn't like that from the first, but it was a control-
lable dislike. At first none of the questions they asked him
or the answers he gave seemed especially important. What
bothered him about them then was that the questioning
to so large an extent seemed to be inspired by Les Gilman's
statements. He didn't like Gilman. He'd never liked Gilman. He most particularly disliked this situation in which
Gilman could pretend to so intimate and detailed a
knowledge of Bob Herman's business.

But then the questioning persisted. It didn't matter
whether they were being angry and threatening with him
or kindly and patient. Either way they kept pressing him.
Neither their harshness nor their friendliness had much
effect on Bob. He was Wonderboy and he could take it.
Hints of how they might rough him up if they lost patience
with him rather amused him. He wasn't frightened of
them.

The other intervals, when their patience seemed in-
exhaustible and they went on and on talking to him for
his own good, did nothing but confuse him. He was willing enough to go along with them. By nature he was not
unobliging, but what they wanted of him was for him to
tell them what he thought about things he did and how
he felt about things he did, and they wouldn't understand
that a man did things without thinking and that sometimes he felt good and other times he felt bad but most
of the time he must have been feeling just all right or
maybe wasn't feeling at all because he couldn't remember
how he felt those times.

They kept telling him he had to remember, and they
prodded his memory by throwing at him again and again

things they had from Gilman. With every repetition Bob's rage against Gilman grew till he was literally speechless with it. Automatically his hands balled into fists. His chin dropped toward his chest. His demeanor so clearly reflected his intention that the detectives warned him to behave and they moved between him and Gilman.

Then they had Les out of there and Bob was alone with them; but, if anything, they were pressing him harder then.

"You were around here all the time?"

"I used to come around."

"All the time?"

"Not all the time. I'm at the gym all the time. I got to keep my training up."

"When you weren't at the gym, you were here all the time?"

"No. Not all the time. I'd come around."

"How often did you come around?"

"How do I know how often? I wasn't keeping no count. I'd drop around."

"Every day?"

"Sometimes I'd miss a day."

"How often did you miss days?"

"I don't know. Every once in a while I'd miss a day."

"But otherwise you came to see her every day."

"Mostly every day."

"And every night?"

"Sometimes I'd get around here in the daytime and sometimes at night. It's not like I had any regular time."

"You didn't spend your nights here?"

"No."

"You weren't living here with her?"

"No. I've got my own place. I've got me this room."

"But she was your girl?"

"No."

"You've got another girl?"

"No."

"Then she was your girl."

"No. I told you no."

"You came over here every day. What did you do when you came over here?"

"It wasn't every day."

"Mostly it was."

"Yeah, mostly. But not every day."

"What did you do over here?"

"We had some drinks. We had laughs. She was a lot of laughs."

"And a healthy boy like you, he don't want anything but laughs. You wouldn't be queer now, kid, would you?"

Not all questions are alike. There are questions that seek answers. They are probes after information. Then there are other questions, the ones that are designed only to provoke a response. The detectives working on Bob were past looking for information. They were satisfied that they had all the answers. Before they had come this far in their interrogation of Bob they were convinced that they had their case made. On the material evidence, on Les Gilman's testimony, and on Bob's own admissions they had him. In their eyes it was open and shut. Bob Herman was their man.

With this questioning they were trying only to break him down and bring him to a state where he would make damaging admissions. They were pelting him with questions that carried built-in responses. They knew that he would fight off a suggestion of homosexuality with more passion than he could ever bring to denying murder because they knew which in his system of values would be the more abhorrent. The question was designed to put Bob off balance. It was asked with that sole purpose. Inevitably it worked. With Bob, already worried about questioning that to him seemed totally inspired by what

Les Gilman had been saying of him, it could not but work.

"He say that?" Bob asked. "He say I'm a fag?"

"Nobody said anything, nobody but you, kid. You say you hang around this woman all the time and you say it's just for laughs."

"I was looking out for her, taking care of her like."

"Taking care of her like. Like what?"

"Like she was always drinking too much. She hardly ate at all unless it was I was eating with her, and even then she didn't eat much. She was always leaving her door unlocked. She needed somebody he should take care of her like."

"Like a father."

Bob knew they were making fun of him when they said that. If it hadn't been that he so much didn't feel like laughing, he would have laughed. It was such a crazy way of describing how it had been with him and Claire. He might have said like a friend, but he didn't know how to say it. He said nothing.

"You want to tell us you weren't laying her?"

"I didn't say I wasn't. Some of the time I was."

"That's better. There's nothing wrong with that. It's nature. You were getting it, and then you weren't getting it any more. What happened? What stopped it?"

"Nothing happened. It didn't stop."

"Then you were laying her all the time?"

"No, not all the time. Mostly it was we'd have some drinks and we'd have a lot of laughs. Mostly she didn't want to."

"Mostly she didn't want to, but you did?"

"Sometimes I did."

"Whether she wanted to or not?"

"It wasn't like that. Mostly she didn't want anything but drinks. It was like she never wanted to sober up. It was all right for her. Anyhow I guess it was, but I can't drink the way she drank, not and keep in shape I can't. She got passed-out drunk. Every day she got passed-out drunk. If I got passed-out drunk every day, I'd be washed up in no time. I couldn't drink the way she drank, and I didn't want to."

"But you did want to lay her even when she was drunk?"

"Not always. Mostly I didn't. Sometimes she was feeling a little that way, and then we would. Most times she said she had her drinking to do and to hell with me and to hell with my dick."

"Tell us about those times, kid. What did you do to her those times?"

"I didn't do nothing to her those times."

"She said the hell with you and the hell with your dick and you just let her get away with it?"

"You don't know the way she would say it. It was a laugh the way she said it."

"And you'd just as soon laugh as screw. You're sure you're not a queer?"

Bob did want to explain it, but he had never before tried. He'd never even thought to explain it to himself.

"Sometimes we did both," he said.

"Both what?"

"Laughed and screwed, that's what."

"Most studs, a dame said something like that to them, they'd slap her in the mouth."

"I don't slap no dames, and anyway that wasn't the way she said it."

"How did you like it better, kid, having her while you were having those laughs, or waiting till she was passed out and mounting her then?"

"I never."

"You never what?"

"I never touched her when she was passed out."

"The first day you ever saw her. She was passed out on

the sofa and you were on the sofa with her with your hands up under her skirt."

"I wasn't mounting her. Nobody said I was mounting her. What do you think I am? Some kind of an animal maybe with them moving men coming by all the time?"

"That's what we're trying to find out, kid. What are you?"

"How do you mean, what am I?"

"Tell us about that time. What were you doing with your hands up under her skirt?"

"Nothing. I wasn't doing nothing."

"Just keeping your hands warm?"

"It wasn't a cold day."

Then they'd make a switch to the last night he'd seen her.

"Tuesday night. How was she Tuesday night?"

"She was all right. She was like always."

"Drinks and laughs?"

"Yeah, like always."

"But Tuesday night she passed out on you. That wasn't like always, was it?"

"It happened that way a lot of times. Even the first time I was ever here, the day she was moving in, it happened like that. He told you how it was."

"Never mind what he told us. We want you to tell us."

"Yeah, never mind what he told you. You've been paying him plenty of mind. Whatever that shithead said, you wasn't telling him no never mind."

"She passed out on you Tuesday night."

"Like she done a lot of other times."

"What made Tuesday night different then?"

"It wasn't no different. It was like a lot of other times."

"All right. It was like a lot of other times, but some of the times you came up here, she didn't pass out on you. What made those times different?"

"Nothing made them different. They weren't any different."

"Now, look, kid. You think you're talking to your grandmother maybe? You think you're talking to a couple of punks who don't know the score? You're talking to us. So now we'll start over again."

"Nothing to start on. Nothing was different."

"You're a guy. She's a dame. You come up here and you want to get her in bed. Sometimes you come up here and you do. Sometimes she gets passed out and you can go home and play with yourself. You want to tell us it's no different a day you get yourself a piece and a day you're not getting anything?"

Bob pulled himself together and tried to make them understand. "You got to know what she was like," he said. "She drank all the time. All the time she drank till she was passed out. Come up here any day and she's drinking and nothing ever stops her drinking till she's passed out. It's always the same."

"That's not what you've been telling us."

"Yes, it is."

"You've been telling us sometimes she passed out on you and sometimes she didn't."

"She did or she didn't, she was no different. It was me, not her."

"Okay. It was you. Tell us about yourself, boy."

"What about me?"

It was long and it was laborious. Possibly even if they had given Bob time to think, he wouldn't have been able to put it into words, but they didn't give him time to think. Mostly they shot the questions at him so fast and from so many angles that he didn't even get to speak the few words he had, much less think up any better ones.

Certainly this bit of it was clear enough to him. For Claire Burns each of her days came to the same sort of end. She drank and she went on drinking till the liquor took hold and the glass fell out of her hand. Whether Bob stayed with her till she passed out or whether he left her before she'd reached that daily goal would make no real difference to her.

With him or without him, she always reached it. Whether he stayed around for it or not was his choice, not hers. There'd been the times when he had other things he had to do and, when the time came he had to take off, he would take off and leave her to go on with her drinking alone. Times he had nothing else to do he stayed with her. It was as uncomplicated as that. She never had anything else to do. Her life had been that much simpler. She was always free to work at her drinking.

The trouble was they persisted in mixing the two things up together when, the way it had been with her and Bob, the two things had never been mixed up at all. It had never been that sometimes they made love and sometimes she drank till she passed out, leaving him deprived. He'd tried to explain it to them. He'd tried to make them understand that he hadn't always been hanging around with the thought of taking her to bed.

He'd been up to her place so much because she was good company. He liked her and he was concerned for her. There had been the times when, being with her, he did come to want her, and most of those times he had her, but when he'd tried to make them understand that it wasn't every time he came to her place, he came with that in his head, they started up with this talk about his being a queer.

Bob preferred to let them think he'd been having her all the time. After all, they did keep telling him having lead in his pencil was nothing to be ashamed of. It was just nature. Anything else was queer.

They kept after him about it, again and again. They

might circle around it for a while but they always came back to the same center. Eventually they had him saying he wanted her all the time and he wasn't having her all the time.

"And Tuesday night, boy. Did you get any before she passed out on you Tuesday night?"

He could have told them that somehow Tuesday hadn't been that kind of a night. It had been one of the times when he hadn't even felt like making a pass at her. He told himself that saying it would just start up the queer talk again. He'd had enough of that.

"No," he said. "I didn't get any Tuesday night."

"That was the first time you were here. The second time—what about it the second time? You came back then and you put it to her."

"I didn't."

"You did come back?"

"I don't know I came back. What would I come back for?"

"You just told us what for. Don't try to kid us about that now."

"She was passed out. I locked the door for her and I went out of here. If I came back, I couldn't get in. She was passed out, so she couldn't get up and let me in; and I'd locked the door so, if I came back, I couldn't get in."

"Some guy got in. Why wasn't it you?"

"Look. If I came back, it wasn't for that. If I came back at all, if was for my jacket."

"What jacket?"

"My jacket. I forgot my jacket when I was here Tuesday. I left it there on the chair. I don't know I came back; but, if I did, it was for that."

One of the detectives picked the jacket off the chair and held it up.

"This jacket?"

"Yeah. My jacket."

"This is your jacket?"

"Of course, it's my jacket. I left it here. There was nobody else here. You can ask anybody is it my jacket. Everybody's seen me wearing it."

"'THERE WAS NOBODY ELSE HERE.' You said that. 'THERE WAS NOBODY ELSE HERE.' Now we're getting somewhere, boy."

"I mean there was nobody else here when I left the jacket, when I put her on the bed and I locked the door and I went out of here."

"And when you came back? Was there anybody else here when you came back?"

"I didn't get in when I came back. I couldn't get in. I'd locked the door."

"And you had no key?"

"I been telling you. I never had no key."

"What's this the key to?"

"What key?"

They held the key up. They waved it in front of him.

"This key," they told him. "The key you had in your jacket pocket."

"Not in my jacket pocket. I never carry no keys in my jacket pocket. I always have my key in the pocket of my pants."

He brought his key out and showed them. It was the key to his room and all the key he'd ever had.

"And this key in your jacket pocket? You don't know what that one is?"

"It ain't mine. I just got the one, the key to my room. That other one, it ain't mine."

"Whose is it then?"

"I don't know. It ain't mine. I never had it."

They took him to the door and they tried it in the lock. They searched the apartment and they found its mate. On

the cupboard shelf they found the old lock and the key
that went with it, the key that was the mate to the one Les
Gilman had. It gave them a new line of questions to push
at Bob.

Working in pairs, team after team of detectives drove
at him. Why did he switch the locks? Where did he get the
lock? What was this thing he had with locks? Was it like
burying a woman maybe, locking her away so nobody could
get at her?

Where was he the night Emily Wilson died? Was that
the first time he put in a lock? Were there others? How
many? Where? How long had he been doing this?

They even tried to make him show them how he did it,
wanting him to act out slapping the tape on their mouths.
They knew that, when they would have their man for the
one killing, they would have him for both. They didn't tell
Bob how they knew, only that they did know.

The microscope boys in the police lab pinned that down
for them. When the Medical Examiner removed from
Claire's mouth the strip of tape, revealing her lips lacerated
from straining against it, that bit of tape had gone to the
lab. Under the microscope small irregularities of weave
showed up. The two pieces of tape, the one taken from
Emily Wilson and the one taken from Claire Burns, were
consecutive pieces cut from the same roll.

VIII

Bob Herman never was clear in his mind which were the detectives and which the psychiatrists. While the one came at him in pairs and the other came at him singly, it seemed to him that the psychiatrists were detectives who were so good at it that they could send him into an aching, blind confusion without the assistance of any partner.

Maybe they did ask different sorts of questions, but to Bob there was no difference. The detectives wanted to know what kind of a thing he had with locks. The ones that came at him alone wanted to know if he did something dirty with keys. They knew what he did when they had him locked up and he was by himself. They asked him if he saw people in the cell with him. They asked him if he was afraid of these people they wanted him to say he saw.

When he said he saw nobody and he wasn't afraid of anyone, they told him how he moved about throwing punches. They asked him about his footwork, except that they didn't call it footwork. They called it his dancing and they wanted to know if he always took the same number of steps. If it was three steps, they asked him if it had to be three. Did he ever take nine? Didn't he ever feel he had to take three steps times three?

If Bob was unable to comprehend what the detectives were after, he was even less able to understand what the psychiatrists wanted of him. To the detectives he was the rapist-killer to be cajoled, tricked, and coerced into handing them the leads they needed for picking up those bits of additional evidence they would have to have if first the District Attorney's office and later a judge and jury were to be satisfied beyond a reasonable doubt. It is the rare precinct detective who considers reasonable doubt to be anything but an aspect of the administration of justice slipped in there some time by some cop hater just to make a detective's job harder than it had to be. The men who were working on Bob Herman included no rarity of such stripe.

To the psychiatrists, Bob was a man accused of rape and murder, all but caught in the act in one case and prime suspect in another. No one was asking the psychiatrists for a judgment of his guilt or innocence. Their job was to determine whether under the legal definition of insanity this man was sufficiently sane to stand trial for the insane crimes he was accused of committing.

It was not that they didn't know that he shadowboxed and practiced his footwork. It was their job to determine that the shadowboxing and the footwork were no more than they seemed on the surface and that they neither masked nor reflected pathological compulsions.

So to Bob their questions had to sound crazy as did the questions about the locks. There were other questions as well. They asked him about his mother. Did he like his mother? How much did he like her? Very much? Did he like her more than anybody else in the world? Did he like her so much that it made him hate everybody else? When they weren't asking him that, they wanted to know did he hate his mother.

Those also were crazy questions, but they weren't any crazier than the questions about mounting women and killing women and then locking these women away. It wasn't just Claire. It was the other one as well, and they wouldn't believe he'd never even known her, not any more than just to hear about her after she was dead. Even if he just told them he hadn't ever seen that other woman, they came back at him with the talk about how maybe he was a queer.

The crazy, twisted way they came at him about the things that were was bad enough. He'd had a mother. He'd known Claire. He'd heard about this other woman who'd been in the apartment before Claire came, and he'd heard the tale of what had been done to this other woman and how she died. He'd heard about how she had the extra lock put on her door and then, while it was still brand new, before she even had a chance to give that shithead super over there a key to it, she'd been dead.

He knew his jacket and he knew they found a key to Claire's new lock in the pocket. He even knew that again, as it had been with the other woman in the apartment, somehow Claire's death was also mixed up with the lock on her apartment door. There'd been all those times when the door hadn't been locked at all, when anyone could walk in, and none of those times had anything happened to her. Then there'd been the other times when he had been around and looking after her and he'd seen to it that the door was locked behind him.

They kept telling him that the stud who killed that Wilson dame had a key to the lock. They kept asking him what kind of a dope he was, locking the door on that lock and thinking he was keeping her safe. If a stud who went raping and killing had a key to the lock, then locking the door didn't keep her safe at all. It just kept her safe from everybody but this one stud who raped and killed, and what would be the sense in that?

"She was yours," they kept telling him. "You were keeping her safe for the time when you'd be having this yen of yours to knock her off. Every chance you got, you locked her up so she'd be there for you when you were ready. Don't try to tell us you had her locked up all the time, keeping her safe for some other stud, and you say you don't even know him."

When they put it that way, he had to admit he didn't know why he'd been locking the door after him every time he left the apartment. He knew his reason wasn't anything like what they were trying to make him say it was, but he couldn't tell them or even himself what it was like. A man never has a reason for locking doors. Locks are for locking. A man locks them.

There wasn't any of them who would accept that. The ones who came at him singly and the ones who worked him over in pairs seemed completely of a mind on that. There had to be a reason for everything, like the footwork, even, and the shadowboxing. They kept asking him why he was always doing it. Okay, he could tell them. For the footwork and the shadowboxing he did have a reason and he knew what it was. He had to keep himself in shape and he had to keep his timing sharp. A man didn't work on it all the time, he went off quicker than you'd think.

There'd always been this reason and it'd always been all the reason he needed. It was the reason accepted by everyone he ever knew, the studs around the gym, the managers, the trainers, even cops. Take Frankie Giordano, for instance. Even people who never knew anything about it, people like Claire, to them it had seemed a good enough reason. But now they kept wanting out of him some second reason and it had to be crazy, like seeing people who weren't there and wanting to beat up on them or thinking about people he hated like his mother. Or did he love his mother?

Actually it was the psychiatrists who kept after him about his shadowboxing and the detectives who worked on why he kept locking that door, but he soon reached the place where to him one question seemed much like another. All of them seemed to end in the same place.

"Why? Was it for love or was it for hate?"

Bob knew the words, but they'd never held much meaning for him. He'd never in his life said to anyone, "I love you." He also never in his life had said to anyone, "I hate you." He never thought of people that way. A friendly sort of boy, he'd always liked people and he was liked by them. In his world there were people, and people were all right. There were also a few shitheads, and they were no good. If you asked Bob what was wrong with them, he'd never be able to tell you. They were just no good. It was as simple as that.

He expected nothing good of them and they never surprised him. In their presence he automatically bristled with hostility, and it isn't often you'll find a man who takes kindly to that. Occasionally perhaps there'd been someone who did try to reach the boy, making friendly overtures, seeking some fissure in his armor of belligerence.

It was never a success. Once he had categorized a man, nothing would change his judgment.

"Shitheads don't fool me," he would tell himself, "not even when they come sucking around."

If there'd been nothing else to make the questioning seem blind and crazy, the way he felt about the people who fired the questions at him would have been enough to keep him off balance. They were people, all of them, even the ones who were tough and threatening and the ones who never let him know how they were going to be, keeping him dizzy with their rapid and sudden shifts from warm friendliness to angry threat and back to friendliness again.

They were giving him a hard time. Nobody had ever given Bob Herman a harder time. Still, whatever the provocation, he never thought of them as shitheads. They were people and he was always prepared to like them, just as he invariably liked the fighters matched with him in the ring. Not all of his fights had been easy ones. It wasn't every fight he could come out of unhurt, but even in the worst of his fights he never had a moment of not liking his opponent or of not being ready to come out of the ring and call the man his friend.

Furthermore, he couldn't remember any opponent who hadn't felt the same way about him. He had no way of understanding why all this should be so different. He wasn't sucking up to anybody. He never had and he wouldn't know how; but they were people and he did want to be friendly. He wanted to help. He was eager to please. He wasn't trying to snow anybody. He wasn't trying to pretend to be anything he wasn't or to get away with anything he'd done. He'd always been a good guy and he was still a good guy. Why didn't any of these people like him?

That they didn't was obvious. The best he had from any of them was nothing like friendliness. He had no words for what someone more articulate might have called a surface affability used to cover over pity. All he knew was that, however much it might seem friendly, it wasn't; and whatever it was, it was no good to him, whether as something that might help him out of his predicament or even as something that might in even the smallest measure alleviate the loneliness of it.

Locked up as he was and chivied incessantly by the relays of questioners, he wasn't seeing those people he knew before and whom he called his friends. Whether they weren't permitted to get to him or they didn't care to come he didn't know. People always liked him and now people didn't any more.

Why should he think his old friends would be any different from all these detective people and psychiatrist people and he didn't know what all. He couldn't get it out of his head that, if things were as they always had been, these new people, the detectives and the psychiatrists, would have been prone to like him. They would have been his friends.

He saw only two people he'd known before. There was Frankie Giordano and he'd been sort of a friend, not as close as the studs around the gym, but almost. Yet in just the couple of minutes that day up in Claire's apartment Frankie had changed. One minute he'd been the last of the people Bob had always known, and in the next minute he appeared to Bob as the first of these new people who, when they didn't think he was lying, thought he was so crazy that he didn't know what was from what wasn't.

The second one was his manager. He came, all anger and accusation, talking to Bob as though Bob were a shithead. It was no good trying to answer him or to tell him anything. Bob never came sucking around and he wasn't going to begin now.

So Bob sat with his head down and looked at his hands. He did that a lot these days, looking at his hands. Sometimes, if they left him alone long enough, he would sit for hours that way, examining his hands, turning them first palm up and then palm down, holding them flat, flexing his fingers, clenching into fists and then unclenching. His hands bothered him. They were going so long naked and uncovered that they hardly seemed like his own any more.

Everybody knew the score. No fighter ever did himself any good hitting the juice. It wasn't as though his manager had ever told him anything else but. It wasn't as though he hadn't had all the warnings any boy needed. So now what had he done?

He'd thrown away his whole career. And whatever made him think it was all his to throw away? What about all the time and trouble and expense his manager had put into him? He'd thrown all that away too. The manager wasn't a hard man. He knew that kids were kids and he didn't expect any kid to carry a man's head on him. A kid could

always make a mistake and people understood that, but
Bob wasn't satisfied to make a mistake. Bob was a mistake.
What he was was something a man wouldn't even spit
on. If he wanted a lawyer, his manager would get him one.
Not for anything, he was to understand, but just so no one
could ever say he ran out on anybody, no matter who, no
matter what.

Bob sat trying to recognize his own hands. He let the
words roll over him. More and more he was learning to do
that, taking words as though they were punches and rolling
with them.

"You," the manager barked at him. "You. I'm talking to
you."

"I hear you."

"And don't go getting fresh with me. I asked you
something."

"I heard you."

"So answer me. You want a lawyer? Answer me and
leave me get out of here before I puke."

"Get out of here before you puke," Bob mumbled. "You
got no right to hang around here if you're going to puke.
You'll be making trouble for people having to clean it up
after you."

"All I want out of you is just an answer, yes or no. No
smart cracks, just the answer. You want for me to get you a
lawyer or don't you?"

"I want for you to haul ass out of here and stop bothering me. I don't care if you puke so hard you drag your ass-
hole up to your eyes. You just go do it some place else and
don't come messing with me."

"And that's all the thanks I get?"

"You want thanks. Okay, thanks. Now I said it. You got
what you came for. Take it and scram."

"Look now, boy, you're in no shape to be ordering me
around. You're in no shape to give nobody no orders."

"That's right. I'm in no shape. I'm a mistake. I make you puke. I don't want you puking up no lawyer for me. I don't want no nothing from you. Get the fucking hell out of here and stop taking my time. I got things to do. I got a dame to kill. Don't you want to get out of here and leave me at it?"

"Jesus! What are you?"

"I'm a mistake. I shouldn't have killed no dames. I should have killed cock instead. Managers. I should have killed managers. Boo!"

There was an expression of ferocity Bob had often practiced for use in the ring; but he'd never used it because it wouldn't work with a mouthpiece in, and anyhow he'd never been able to do it without laughing and how far will a fighter get if he goes into the ring for laughs?

Now that he had no mouthpiece in and he didn't feel at all like laughing, he brought it out for the first time. The manager left, but there was no satisfaction in seeing him scuttle away. This was an old friend. They'd liked each other. They'd done all right together, Bob and the manager, but that was all over now. Bob wasn't doing all right with anyone any more, and how could it be that everybody was out of step but him? What had happened? What was it that just in a minute changed everything? Or maybe nothing was changed, nothing but Bob.

The time came when they turned him loose, but it made virtually no difference. The psychiatrists weren't around then. There was no one around to tell him that he had done well with satisfying them of his sanity. He would need to have guessed that he had also done well with the detectives. They weren't telling him. For all the work they had put in on him, for all the success they'd had with confusing him and with jockeying him into saying so many things that they had put into his mouth, those further things they wanted from him which they couldn't put in his mouth, they'd never had from him.

They wanted him to take them to the place where he bought the locks, but they had no trick they could use on him that would make him say he had ever bought any locks. They had been all over the city with his mug shots, but they could find no one who had ever sold him a lock. So the men in the DA's office had looked at the Police evidence and had told the detectives it wasn't enough. More would be needed before a grand jury could be asked to indict. The office case load was too heavy and the court calendars too crowded to permit anyone the luxury of going to trial with an action that carried so poor a possibility of success.

The detectives didn't agree. They felt that they had done brilliantly. They were more than satisfied with their case against Bob Herman. They were convinced that the fault lay with the DA's office and the courts. It was always the way. A man worked his heart out to bring some law and order to the wicked city only to be frustrated at every turn by a lot of bleeding hearts who would never quit yapping about innocent until proved guilty.

So they turned Bob loose; but, no sooner had he shown his face back in the precinct than they let him know where he stood. He wasn't in the clear. They had their eye on him. They would get him yet. Before they were through with him they would have it wrapped around his neck so tight that there wouldn't be a bleeding heart anywhere ready to go to bat for him.

They told him he was guilty until proved innocent and that everything else was a bleeding-heart aberration. That much Bob Herman could understand. That he hadn't been proved guilty didn't matter. He was a man who hadn't been proved innocent. In his world, furthermore, everybody knew as much.

IX

If in jail Bob felt cut off from life as he'd always known it, released he felt no less cut off. It was no good going around to the gym. He could expect no welcome there. There had been that moment up in Claire's apartment when the change came, and he'd dropped out of the world as he'd known it. Now nothing had changed back. If anything, his release made things worse. In jail he was the poor bastard who was going to go up for life for raping and killing two women.

A free man, he became the son-of-a-bitch who was getting away with the rape and murder of two women. The judgment against him still stood but was now unsoftened by pity. It was the way it would have been even if the red-faced and outraged precinct detectives hadn't spread the word.

He had money still coming to him out of his last purse, but he couldn't get that without going around to his old manager and asking for it. That was something he couldn't do. It never entered his mind that he could rightfully demand what was his. In his own thinking he had passed out of the world of men who had rights. It seemed to him that he would not be demanding. He would be asking and asking was the same thing as sucking around.

The rent had run out on his room and when he went around there, he was told it had been rented to someone else. If he wanted his things he could go around to his manager and get them. The manager had picked them up and

he was holding them for Bob. The things were like the
money. Bob would do without them before he'd go sucking around.

It left him without funds, without a place to sleep, without work, and with no more to wear than what he stood up
in, plus one change of shirt, three spare handkerchiefs, and
a couple of changes of socks.

He needed a job, but when he laboriously read down the
columns of help-wanted ads there was nothing people
wanted done that didn't seem beyond him. In most of the
ads he couldn't even understand the job descriptions,
much less contemplate any such undertaking. He tried the
midtown employment agencies along Sixth Avenue and
that was better, insofar as the rows of cards tacked to the
boards alongside the agency doors did make sense to him.

Dishwashers were wanted and porters. He wasn't quite
clear about what porters did. Redcaps in the railroad sta-
tions were porters, and he didn't like the sound of that.
He wasn't ready to take on anything where he would be
working for tips. It seemed to him that it would be making
a whole life of sucking around.

Dishwashing seemed better. He could do that. He worked
hard at keeping his mind on reading the cards. As soon as
he looked beyond them, he wanted to run. The whole
district repelled him. The men who stood shoulder to
shoulder with him looking at the cards and the men waiting inside to give out the jobs seemed equally to belong to
the world he had always avoided. This was the world of the
shitheads and, however much he reminded himself that
since that moment in Claire's apartment he had become a
part of this world, he couldn't teach himself to feel at
home in it.

A wispy youth with much matted black beard cocked
a sardonic eye at him.

"Porter or dishwasher," the youth chanted, making a

tuneless song of it, "dishwasher or porter. What's the odds? Either way, we'll be making it a sweeter and better and cleaner world. Porter or dishwasher, brother, which will it be?"

"Porter," Bob mumbled, trying to understand the song. "That's carrying suitcases and stuff, isn't it?"

A short, barking laugh made the beard flap.

"A scholarly type," the beard chortled. "A Latinist even. Walking through life down the road of pure linguistics. Porter—one who carries, a bearer of burdens. Support, export, report, import, all from that same dread root that makes of man a pack animal. And how did the bearer of burdens come to this—the building porter? He who carries the broom? The bearer of the mop and pail? No, brother, this is the Avenue of the Americas. We speak no Latin here. Porters creep out when the better people have gone. They come with their brooms and their mops and they clean up the messes the better people leave. The gob of spittle; the crumpled gum wrapper; the chewed-out, spewed-out gum; the burned-out match; the Tampax ends of the smoked-out filter cigarettes. Such are the burdens these porters bear."

The spate of words washed over Bob, but he caught enough of them for some understanding. He remembered the punchy old man who shuffled through the gym cleaning up after the fighters when it came to closing time. He was called the porter and it could happen to anybody. It came of staying in there too long taking too many hard rights, and that was nothing to be ashamed of because you stayed in there as long as you had to and you took as much as you had to and, if it turned out to be too long and too much, it wasn't any fault of yours.

His picture of the old man didn't bother him, but he had no time to dwell on it since it was quickly replaced by a picture of Les Gilman—Bob had seen him some of the times he'd dropped in on Claire, and Gilman had been mopping the halls.

"Dishwasher," Bob growled. "That's for me. Dishwasher."

"Snob," the beard snorted. "Body snob. Clean-living youth who can take a Board of Health checkup. No syph, no clap, no TB. TB, you're out. VD, you're out. BVDs, boy, you're in."

Bob didn't know what the hell the jerkoff was singing about but he knew the song was offensive.

"Shithead," he snarled and stamped into the office to bark out his demand for a dishwashing job.

He didn't last more than a couple of days, only as long as he remained an anonymous pair of hands, dropping sweat in his private cloud of steam. What tore it was the detectives. It took them only the couple of days to find him on his job. They stood cool and surveyed him in his sweat as they reminded him that they had their eye on him and they were waiting.

Not long after their visit the boss came back to the kitchen and told him to pick up his pay. Perhaps he expected Bob to ask him why, since he had no way of knowing that asking why would be another form of sucking around and Bob wasn't ready for that yet. He didn't wait for Bob to ask. He told him.

"I got all these waitresses working," he said. "The word's getting around already. Five minutes more, they'll all be scared out of here. It's you or it's them."

"Okay," Bob said. "Okay."

Mechanically he went on with his work.

"Don't wait to finish any of that," the man said. "Just drop it where you are. Out. Out right now."

Bob had been moving a stack of plates to the sink. He jerked his hands apart and the stack of plates shattered on the floor at the man's feet.

"Okay," Bob said.

"Son-of-a-bitch," the man screamed. "That comes out of your pay."

"Okay," Bob said.

The first day he'd been in the job, he rented himself a room, paying a week's rent in advance. So he had a place he could go and sleep. He slept long and heavily, never opening his eyes till long after the hot-water pucker had smoothed away from the skin on his fingers and long after the smell of the steam and the dishwater had aired out of his shirt and pants.

He intended to sleep out the week of his room rent, putting off until after that even beginning to think about what he would do next. He found, however, that he couldn't sleep that long and, once he was awake, he couldn't stay long in his room. It made him feel more imprisoned than he'd ever felt under detention.

He took to the streets, beginning by wandering into quarters of the town he'd never previously frequented. Soon the loneliness of that drove him back to the streets he'd always known, and he wandered those disconsolately. Like a drunk who has taken the pledge and walks compulsively back and forth past what had been his favorite saloon, Bob gravitated alternately to the twin poles of the gym and the building where Claire had lived. In his approach to either place he would crawl along; but, once he was abreast of either, he hurried his steps, getting himself away before he might break down and go in.

It was inevitable that in these walks of his he would again and again run into Frankie Giordano. Each time he tried to go by without speaking, but each time Giordano did speak and bit by bit Bob softened to the point of first returning the policeman's greetings and later even stopping for a few words of chat. When Giordano spoke to him, it was as though there had never been that moment of change up in Claire's apartment. Bob could have yielded to it and allowed himself the pleasure of feeling like a man again, but he was too wary for that.

He had come to live in a world of traps, and Frankie's easy friendliness was not to be trusted. It would be only another trap. Giordano put it to him.

"You think I'm a louse," he said.

Bob hadn't been thinking it, but he didn't know how to put into words what he had been thinking. He felt that somehow, by some agency he could never hope to understand, he'd lost his right to make judgments on anybody. Who was he to have any opinion of Patrolman Frank Giordano? He knew or he thought he knew what Giordano thought of him; and in the face of that to pass by with more than the briefest grunt of salutation would be another variety of sucking around.

"Nah," he said. "You're all right."

"I didn't do anything I didn't have to do, kid."

"Yeah. I know that."

"But that doesn't stop you being sore. I can understand that."

"I ain't sore about anything."

"You see," Giordano tried to explain, "you looked bad. It wasn't my fault you looked bad and it wasn't yours either, but I can't ever let that stop me from doing my job."

"Yeah. I know. You got your eye on me."

"What makes you say that?"

"I know the score. That much I know the score."

"You don't know anything, kid."

"I know the score."

"If you think I'm going around laying for you, you don't know anything."

"You just got to do your job."

"Laying for you, that ain't my job."

"It's okay. I know it can't be no different."

He started to move off. Giordano took him by the arm and held him. The old Bob Herman would at least have tried to shake off Giordano's hand. Now Bob just stood, waiting for what might come next.

"You're innocent till you're proved guilty," Giordano told him. "That's the way we do it in this country. You're innocent till you're up in court and they prove you guilty. Nobody has the right to say you're guilty till you've been in court and up before a jury and they hear everything about you and about what happened and they think about it and they say you're guilty. It's got to be like that. Twelve men in a court and hearing the whole thing and making up their twelve minds. I'm no twelve men, kid. I'm just one cop."

"And you think I sneaked up on her when she was passed-out drunk and I screwed her and I killed her."

"I think somebody did it and, the way it all was, it made you look bad. That's not thinking you did it."

"Then maybe you're the only one doesn't think I did."

"I didn't get you turned loose. The DA did, and he's a lot smarter than you or me we'll ever be. He had you turned loose because you're innocent until he proves you guilty, and the way you look to him you don't even look so bad that he wants to try to prove you're guilty. Insufficient evidence. That's what insufficient evidence means, kid."

"What insufficient evidence means," Bob said, for once so articulate that he startled even himself, "is you all keep your eye on me till I do something to make it enough evidence."

Giordano would have liked to deny it, but Giordano was an honest man and he knew what the sentiment was in the detectives' squad room back at the station house.

"Or," he said, "it means people'll have their eye on you until enough time passes without you doing anything. Then they'll stop looking at you."

"How long's that?"

"Gee, kid. I don't know how long. You behave yourself and it won't maybe be too long."

"I'm behaving myself," Bob said and moved off.

Giordano let him go, but Bob was not out of Giordano's mind, and Giordano was a good cop who knew his district. As the opportunity arose, he asked a few questions and again, as the opportunity arose, he dropped a word here and there.

Within a day things happened. A job came Bob's way without his even looking for it, and it came before the week ran out on his room. There was a bar in the neighborhood. It was a quiet bar, run by a quiet man. What seemed like a very long time before, Bob had been in the habit of dropping around to this bar for the occasional beer. It was the kind of place that had customers who knew the fight game. They weren't insiders and they weren't the ringside-seat kind. They were two-dollar bettors with wives and kids; and some of them, when they'd meet Bob on the street, used to bring grandsons up to shake hands.

Bob, of course, hadn't so much as been near the place since that day when things had changed for him. He had, in fact, not been in there for some time before that. Once he took up with Claire Burns and began drinking with her, it had come to more drinking than Bob ever needed. There'd been no room for even the most occasional beer.

Then the day after he had the encounter with Frank Giordano he had a second encounter. It was a Sunday morning and he was again out in the streets, drifting compulsively between his two poles of attraction, the gym and the place where Claire had lived. The quiet man who ran this quiet and pleasant bar picked Bob up, as with lingering steps Bob was pushing himself past the gym. The man made the encounter seem accidental. He was careful not to mention that Frankie Giordano had spoken to him.

"Hi, kid," the man said.

"Hi, Grady," Bob answered and walked faster.

Grady came after him. "What did I do?" he asked. "What's eating on you?"

"You ain't done nothing. I said hi, didn't I?"

"You said hi. That's a big deal. You ain't seen a friend for a long time and you say hi. Why ain't you been around to the place?"

"What for? So I can lose you customers?"

"Look. I got friends. They done time. Not like you, they was tried and they was found guilty. They done their time. They're loose. It's like that and they come in and I stand them a drink. It's like to welcome them back and it never lost me no customers."

Bob laughed bitterly. "A stud," he said. "He goes around murdering dames. He's tried. He's found guilty. He don't get loose he can come around you should buy him a drink."

"So you're loose. So you ain't the guy who murdered them babes. They had every detective in town trying to prove it on you and they couldn't prove nothing. So what's that got to mean?"

"It's got to mean they still got their eye on me."

"They got their eye on your ass," Grady scoffed. "It's got to mean you're okay. If it didn't mean you're okay, it's got to mean you're that much smarter than all the detectives in town, which you ain't. Deny that."

Being Sunday morning, it was well before opening time; but they went in and sat in the back room and drank coffee and Grady said he needed a man. Bob insisted Grady didn't need him. Nobody needed him. He wasn't denying Grady's argument, but he kept telling Grady that nobody else thought the way Grady thought.

They kicked it around until it was almost time to open

up. Grady did concede that for a while anyhow it mightn't be good for business if Bob was around the bar during working hours. That, however, didn't change his story about needing a man.

Grady didn't like the way things were going in the neighborhood. It wasn't as though he were like a lot of saloonkeepers who lived upstairs over the bar. Once Grady locked up and went home, he never had an easy moment. All the time he should have been sleeping he worried maybe some of these punks you had around these days were breaking into the bar.

Now if he could have a man to sleep on a cot in the storeroom. It was a nice, airy storeroom, and it could be fixed up a little to make a man comfortable in there. With a good man like Bob sleeping in the storeroom, Grady could go home nights and get some rest.

Grady was careful not to pitch it too strong. He didn't say Bob would be doing him a favor. He just put it as an arrangement by which they could both benefit. He needed a man who could handle himself and who wouldn't be scared of anybody. He also needed a man who could be locked up alone in a saloon and not run wild through the bar stocks.

"A kid who'll be any good to me and who I can be sure ain't no lush," Grady said. "Tell me where I should go find a kid like that."

"I been drinking more than I used to," Bob said.

"I know all about that. It don't make you no kind of a lush. Let me worry about your drinking."

"The way things been going," Bob confessed, "I could use a flop I'd be getting rent free."

Grady moved in fast. "I can't pay you much," he said, "but you get your bed and you get your board and you'll have a couple of bucks for razor blades and a movie and nothing to keep you from having a daytime job along with it. Then, as soon as you get another fight and all the squirts around town see you're still the guy who took Colzano, you'll see quick enough how good you'll be for business."

"I won't be fighting no more," Bob mumbled, reminded of his manager.

"That'll be the day," Grady laughed. Bob left it at that.

They made the deal. It was the answer to where Bob would go now that his week's room rent was running out, and it was an answer Bob liked better than having another try with the notice boards outside the agencies along the Avenue of the Americas.

It wasn't perfect. There was the night Bob turned up about ten minutes before Grady locked up. Bob went straight through to his back room, but in passing he saw the looks the few late customers sneaked at him. After that he was careful to wait outside till the last customer had gone and Grady was turning the lock in the door.

The second night he slept in the storeroom he came in and found a stack of stuff neatly piled on his cot. It was everything he'd had in his old room, the place where he'd been living before he was arrested. It was also all the stuff out of his locker at the gym. On the top of the pile was a check. It was drawn to Bob Herman and signed by his old manager.

He went out to the front where he found Grady shrugging into his coat. Bob gave him a hand with the coat. He was carrying the check with him and he waved it at Grady.

"What's all the crap on my bed?" he asked.

"Your stuff."

"Where did it come from?"

"Where do you think? He was holding it for you."

"And the dough?"

"It's your dough. He was holding that for you, too."

"I don't want nothing from him. I told him I didn't

want nothing from him. I ain't going sucking up to him, and I don't want nobody sucking up to him for me."

"Ever know me to go sucking up to anybody?" Grady growled.

"I don't want nothing out of him," Bob repeated stubbornly.

"It's your stuff and it's your dough. You know me. I'm a business man. I see me a chance to pick myself up a good, young fighter cheap, I don't go passing up no chances. He don't hold your contract any more. I do. And I'm Mike Grady. I got me a kid and my kid's got anything coming to him, I see he gets it. How long do you think I'd stay in business if it wasn't like that? The word gets around Mike Grady can be kicked around or Mike's boy can be kicked around, where am I? Don't be no dumber than you got to be, kid."

Bob wanted to say thanks, but he didn't know how. Instead he grinned and threw a playful punch at Grady's shoulder. Grady grinned right back at him and they sparred around for a couple of moments. Bob went back to his cot, trying to remember how long it had been since he'd last felt that good.

Without ever saying any more about it to Bob, Grady did work at getting him a match, but it was hopeless. Nobody was touching his boy. There was, therefore, little change in Bob's day-to-day routine. He took over the job of cleaning up the bar after Grady locked up. He slept in the storeroom. He always had a good meal in the locked-up saloon when he came in at night; and one of the things Grady always did when he was readying things in the morning for opening up was push a hearty breakfast into Bob.

When Bob got himself out of the place before the first early customer turned up, Grady never said anything; and Grady never asked why Bob always stayed away until just after the last customer was gone. Grady knew the looks that passed along the bar that one time Bob came in a few minutes early. More than that, he heard the cracks exchanged the minute the storeroom door closed behind the boy. He wanted to argue, but he said nothing. A good barman doesn't argue with the customers, not about anything important. A friendly dispute about how many games the 1926 World Series went was allowable, but nothing that bit deeper than that.

Bob didn't take on any daytime job. It would have meant going back to the employment agencies and he spared himself even thinking about that. He was a fighter again. He had a manager. Sooner or later he would be getting fights again. If he had been forced to look at himself squarely, he would have known that he didn't believe it, but there was no necessity.

He had his bed, a corner where he could keep his stuff, and those two big meals a day. If in between he was hungry, Grady was giving him enough so he could always go for a hamburger and a glass of milk at some counter place where nobody talked to him and he talked to nobody. His check Grady banked for him, and the money was there for when he would need it. That would be some day when his shoes wore out or something like that.

Still it was a long day and he had to fill it somehow. When the weather was bad, he would hit a movie early when the house first opened, and he would sit in the balcony. The first couple of times around, he would watch the show, but after that he would sit there just letting it happen in front of him. On good days he would go to the park.

There were always kids in the park playing one kind of pick-up game or another, and Bob could watch that. After a few days the kids in the park came to know him and they accepted him as a fixture. They got him to referee their games and some days when they were an odd number, they'd choose up to see which side would get him. If they ever gave any thought to who he was, they assumed he was some sort of Youth Group worker. He was inflexible about playing fair and sticking to the rules.

It helped toward filling his days, but it didn't fill them. There was always the time when the kids had to go home to their suppers, and, since on the bad days Bob was getting more movies than he wanted, he made it a rule that movies had to be saved for only the bad days.

A good part of his time, therefore, and particularly in the evenings, Bob was on the streets. He worked at varying his routes, but whichever way he went, he would still keep coming back to his two constants, walking slowly past the gym, slowly parading the street where Claire had lived. Obviously he couldn't miss it the first day the apartment-to-let sign was gone from the front of the house.

X

The apartment was a bargain. Since most people wouldn't have the place at any price, H. Conover (Just Call Me Con) Langdon didn't have too much trouble working a deal on it. The deal began in the ordinary enough way. He came around with the New York *Times* ad and looked at the apartment.

It had by then been long enough vacant to be a serious worry to the owners. Whatever they could do to make it more attractive they'd done. The place was freshly painted and decorated, and Les Gilman was authorized to tell prospective tenants that on request the owners would re-paint in any color scheme required.

A new stove and refrigerator had been installed in the kitchen and a new shower-head in the bathroom. Both of the locks had been changed and the management was ready to assure any tenant that nobody but Les Gilman held a key to the apartment. Every window had been fitted with the most efficient locks. Although Gilman wasn't authorized to offer concessions on the rent, he'd been told to suggest to anyone interested that on applica-tion to the office a prospect might find the figure subject to negotiation.

From the first Con Langdon presented himself as a bargain hunter. He went through the place, surveying everything most meticulously, before he so much as asked his first question. As long as he was asking nothing, Les

Gilman volunteered nothing. When Langdon completed his tour of the place, Langdon broke the silence.

"What are they asking for it?" he said.

Gilman came up with as inflated a figure as he dared invent.

Langdon whistled. "I'd be taking it just as is," he said. "I wouldn't be asking them to paint for me or to make any changes or anything."

"It's all been done fresh," Gilman told him. "New paint all over, new stove, new ice box, new plumbing in the bathroom. Everything they gonna do they done."

Langdon looked thoughtful. "But it doesn't really change anything," he murmured.

"It makes it nice and clean," Gilman said.

Langdon gave him a scornful little smile. "So now if he comes a third time, maybe he'll leave fingerprints," he said.

"Who?"

"The man. The sex murderer. The one who's hit here twice and they still haven't caught him."

"Oh, that." Gilman shrugged. "They caught him."

"It wasn't in the papers. It would've been in the papers."

"It was in the papers all right. They caught him, but he's got friends on the cops. They left him go."

"The fighter?"

"Yeah. That Herman. They took him right out of here the day we found the second one, but they left him go. Any day you go to the front windows here you'll see him. He's out there all the time, all the time hanging around."

"The place with the built-in sex murderer," Langdon laughed. "And nothing off the rent for that?"

Gilman studied the man, taking in the little paunch where the belt, a little too tightly drawn, creased it; taking in the thinning, pale hair and the neat precision with which it was spread to cover as much pink scalp as possible. This wasn't a notably big man and it wasn't a man who looked as though he'd ever been tough or fearless. Gilman placed him as somewhere in his early fifties, possibly gone soft with middle age and possibly just showing it in middle age as he wouldn't have shown it earlier. Gilman decided to be friendly.

"Look," he said. "I hadn't ought to be saying this, but anybody he takes this place is crazy. I wouldn't live in it if they was giving it away. The landlord he knows what he's got here. It's the place ain't nobody's gonna want to rent. Cheap rent or high rent, it makes no difference. They might as well go for high because who takes it he's got to be out of his head, and you get a guy he's that crazy, he can be crazy enough to pay what they're asking."

Langdon shrugged. "It's a pity," he said. "I like the place, but I'm not that crazy and I haven't got that kind of dough."

"Yeah," Gilman said sympathetically. "Who has?"

They left the apartment and Gilman carefully locked it behind them. As he was seeing Langdon out of the building, he noticed the man pause to look at the brass plate fastened to the vestibule wall.

Gilman took Langdon by the arm and hurried him toward the street. "Out there," he said. "Going by over there across the street, that's him."

"The fighter?"

"Yeah, him. All the time he's walking by out there. All the time like maybe he was picketing the place. Ever since they turned him loose, I been seeing him out there. Particularly at night I been seeing him."

"And the police don't do anything?"

"He's got friends on the cops. Like I told you, they left him loose."

Langdon sighed. "It's a shame," he said. "It sure is a shame."

He went off and Les Gilman told himself he'd never see that one again, but Langdon went straight to the real estate office and made his deal. He'd always been a shrewd bargainer, but he never went into a bargaining session more securely in the driver's seat.

He was a mild-looking, plump, little man, and he was soft-spoken and mild-mannered. There was nothing in his bearing to indicate that he came to these negotiations completely clear in his mind about how he would proceed and completely confident of his success.

Diffidently he explained his position. He was an Ohio business man in from out of town. The way he had things set up, he'd always made his headquarters at home in Ohio.

"I don't need this New York move," he explained. "I can go on the way I've always done, traveling out of where I am. You see, I don't like taking your time without explaining at the start that I may not even be in the market. At present I'm just exploring the situation."

They were happy to give him the time. They would be delighted to explore the situation with him.

"The way it's been going," he said, "I'm here in New York more than I'm any place else. It's getting so I'm here even more than I'm home and, reading the trend in my line, I can see it's going to be more that way all the time."

He had long been thinking about the move.

"I've looked," he said. "Any time I'm here and I have a little time to kill, I look; but I've just about given up on the idea. I'd like it a lot if I could move Mrs. Langdon here, but your New York rents. If there's no way I can find a place here without giving an arm and a leg for it, we'll just go on the way we've been doing. We're all right there, a nice little town."

They asked him what sort of rental he had in mind.

"Nothing like what you people ask in the ordinary way,"

he answered. "But there's this one apartment you've got in Twelfth Street."

They asked him which apartment.

"That one you're stuck with," he said, sounding never more diffident. "The one you can't rent to anybody since the second woman in there was raped and killed, the one people aren't taking even as a gift."

"We haven't offered to give it away, Mr. Langdon."

"But you're not finding anybody not afraid to take it."

"It's only a matter of time, Mr. Langdon. These things blow over. Another month and there won't be anyone who remembers."

Langdon rose. "You gambling on waiting?" he asked. "Or would you like it off your hands right now?" He named his figure.

"Out of the question."

Langdon started for the door, and they named a figure. He came back and sat down. The bargaining didn't go quickly. Langdon was in no hurry, but eventually they did close the gap between their offers. Langdon had his bargain.

The to-let sign came off the front of the building. The rent was to start the beginning of the following month. Langdon could move in whenever he was ready. If he moved fast enough, he could have the better part of a month rent free.

When they told Les Gilman to take the sign down, he was curious but not worried. Even when they gave him the name of the new tenant, he was still no more than curious. Many people had been in to see the place and always they'd left Les convinced he would never see any of them again. At first they'd come in droves with every thrill seeker in town doing it as a sight-seeing trip.

Among the early ones there'd been nobody seriously looking and even to the last he'd been having a good quota of sight-seers. As time went by, however, there came with the merely curious two other kinds. There were women who were seriously apartment hunting. They came not knowing or having forgotten. Sometimes while they were looking at it, it would come to them where they were. Sometimes they'd like the place and come back later with a friend, and the friend would tell them. Whichever way it was, Les couldn't believe he'd shown the place to any woman who could have gone out of there with even the faintest notion of taking it.

On the other hand, there had been the men. Those who came with wives or spoke of wives gave every evidence of reacting as the single women did. The others, who came alone and gave Les to understand they thought of occupying the place alone or in partnership perhaps with another unattached male, had all had identical reactions to the terms Les quoted to them. A man would have to be a complete fool to take the place at such a price.

So Les was curious. The office told him the apartment would be occupied by Mr. and Mrs. H. Conover Langdon, and he wondered which of the couples he'd shown it to had managed to down their fears of it. He had no misgivings till a few days later, when Mrs. Langdon rang his bell, introduced herself, and asked for the keys. She wanted to measure the windows for curtains and she wanted to look around and see how the furniture was going to fit.

Explaining that she'd just come into town, she was girlishly eager for her first glimpse of her new home. If she hadn't talked about it that way, Les might have thought he'd had a lapse of memory. Since she did introduce herself and since she did go on and on about how exciting it was to be seeing her New York home for the first time, Les knew there was nothing wrong with his memory. This was no one to whom he'd shown the apartment.

He took her upstairs and opened the door for her. In

the apartment he watched her run eagerly from room to room, exclaiming happily over everything, volubly delighted with every detail. She was younger than Wilson was, but older than Burns. She was fatter than either and she was flutteringly coquettish. There had been nothing at all of coquetry in either of the others.

Staying with her in the apartment, Les helped her with her measurements. He found himself feeling at home with her as he'd never felt at home with any other tenant. It wasn't only her friendliness. Nobody could have been friendlier than Claire Burns. It was also her simplicity. Claire's friendliness had always been tainted by her laughter; and, although she never laughed at anyone else nearly as much as she laughed at herself, a man like Les Gilman was deaf to all those other parts of her mirth. He heard her laugh only at him.

This woman was different, not frozen and forbidding like Wilson, not mocking like Burns. Her dress was a little too tight for her and, as she reached upward for her measuring there was a small promise that her breasts might pop up, escaping her bra like balloons released under water.

Les waited for her to give some sign that she knew about the apartment, but she showed nothing. Of the men he thought he'd put off, he wondered which was her husband, and he wondered, further, why he'd heard nothing from the office about the rental he'd been quoting to such prospects and all the other ways he'd misrepresented their offer to every man who had come alone to look at the place.

It seemed impossible that any of the men he'd talked to went to the office and closed a deal for the place without revealing something of the way Les had been showing the apartment. Les, however, had heard nothing from his employers and there lay the complete impossibility. If they'd had even a hint of the way Les had been handling it, he would have heard from them. More than that, he would have been out of a job.

He had to settle for the less incredible of his two impossibilities. The man went from Les to the office and never gave even the smallest hint of what Les had been telling him. Why? What could the man be building? There was a mystery about this somewhere, and Les didn't like it. With these new tenants he'd have to be most specially careful. Something about this was not what it seemed.

Even while he built these suspicions, however, he was watching little, plump Mrs. Langdon and listening to her.

"Tricky," he was thinking. "You got to watch out for them. They're up to something tricky."

He considered the thought and he considered Mrs. Langdon. Try as he would to hang on to his suspicion, he couldn't make himself believe there was anything concealed or devious about this comfortable, little woman. To a more sophisticated eye it would have been obvious at once what there was about her that made her seem so unquestionably honest and open.

It was that all the little, womanly artifices she attempted were uniformly unsuccessful. None of them came off properly. Her hair twisted into a too-tight permanent wave looked more cooked than curled. She had superimposed on her natural mouth a staggeringly unrelated lipstick mouth. Whether she smiled or she spoke or she pouted, her two mouths never seemed to hit on any sort of harmony. The painted one always seemed to be in contradiction of whatever the other was doing.

Even her figure, despite the restraints she put on it, found candid little ways of proclaiming itself. Both at top and bottom her corseting seemed to go just that bit beyond the place where she herself stopped so that every effect of rigidly regimented smooth curvature ended not in a melting curve but in a sharply jutting edge.

This was a woman who might conceivably try to deceive, but it took only a glance at her to know she would never succeed. Everything she was, everything she did, everything she said gave her away.

When Les saw her again, it was a couple of days later, when she moved in. Then she again came alone, explaining she was going to have to call on Les to do for her all the little things a man would ordinarily do in settling the apartment. Mr. Langdon was a traveling man and he wouldn't be back in New York for three more days and wouldn't it be nice if they could have the whole place settled for him before he arrived?

The second day she was in residence Les, coming through the halls in the evening, found her door standing ajar. She was inside, sitting in the living room and she had her chair so placed that she could divide her attention between her television and any traffic that might be passing in the hall. Greeting her, Les offered to shut her door for her.

"No," she told him, "leave it."

Les felt his hackles rise. "Another one," he told himself. "Another one like the crazy Burns babe."

"You're safer with your door locked," he said. "Particularly like now you're here all by yourself you had ought to have the door shut and locked on both the locks. Sitting this way with the door wide open, it ain't safe."

"What is it I've got to be safe from?" she asked.

It could have been one of those mocking questions he remembered Claire Burns asking, but he could find no mockery in the way this one asked it.

"Burglars," he mumbled. "People."

"I like people. I don't like things shut away or locked up. It isn't neighborly. Why back home, back where I come from, nobody hardly ever locks any doors and, when they do, the key's always left under the doormat. Why, it's something everybody does. You never even think about it. You

come to a door and it's only if the weather's bad enough
that you aren't surprised if it's closed. Even then it's never
going to be locked or if it is, you can always look under
the doormat for the key. Anything else would be unfriendly. It would be like serving notice on your neighbors
that you want to keep yourself to yourself. You don't
want anybody dropping by."

More than ever she was making him nervous. Looking
at this woman, watching the way she conducted herself,
listening to her talk, he felt she could hardly have been
more unlike Claire Burns. There was nothing about her
to suggest she was a brave woman, and she was certainly
not the disheveled sort of personality Burns had been.

She was an odd one and Les couldn't put it from his
mind that he had still to see her husband. He had still to
learn which of the men he thought he'd talked off the
place turned out to be so peculiar that he went around
to the office and made his deal and never gave Les away.
There was no reason for the man to do him any favors.
These people had to be up to something.

He fell back on the little notice which by law is fixed
to every apartment door in New York. He read it to her:

"Keep this door closed when not in use. This may save
your life in case of fire."

"I saw that," she said. "I think it's silly."

"If there's a fire, it keeps it from spreading."

"Why should there be a fire?"

"Fires can always happen."

"That's silly."

"It's the law."

"What's the law?"

"Keeping doors locked so fires won't spread if there is
a fire."

"It doesn't say locked. It only says closed."

Reluctantly she closed the door. Les waited in the hall
outside listening for the sound of the locks going home.

He heard nothing. He was mumbling to himself when he went away. This was something he couldn't at all understand. It worried him.

Only a couple of hours later—it was in the evening of the same day—the picture changed, but not so much that it relieved Les Gilman of his worry. The change explained nothing to him. It was instead a fresh shock.

Convinced that the law required her to keep her apartment door closed, Harriet Langdon was carefully law abiding, but she wasn't comfortable with it. Shutting herself away from people was against her nature and contrary to her habits. She had been delighted with the place; but shut up alone in it, she found it was quickly on her nerves. She began thinking up reasons for getting herself out of there. First she thought of something she wanted from the store. She went out for it. She was only a few minutes back from that when she thought of going out to pick up an evening paper. So it went till she'd run out of reasons for going out. Then at every sound in the hall, real or imagined, she took to opening the door and looking out.

Once, when it was a real sound, she came on her next-door neighbor as the woman was letting herself into her own apartment. Harriet saw the keys in her neighbor's hand, and she was fully aware that she'd never seen that door across the hall anything but securely closed. Doggedly she told herself this was only some more of that New York silliness. People, after all, were just folks, and all you had to do was let them know you were just folks as well and that there was always the pot of coffee at the back of the stove and always time any time to sit down with a neighbor and have a little visit.

Flinging her own door wide, she came out into the hall with her hand extended.

"I'm Harriet Langdon," she said. "My husband, Con, and me, we're your new neighbors. We just moved in yesterday."

The woman was startled, but she took the offered hand.

"Yes, I know," she said. "I'm Mrs. Lodge." Wondering whether she should let it sound so much like a rebuff even though the rebuff was intended, she tried again. "Sylvia Lodge," she said. "Do you like your apartment?"

"It's darling. I love it."

"Yes," Mrs. Lodge said lamely.

Harriet pressed on. "All these doors closed and locked," she said. "I just wanted you to know I think it's the silliest, unfriendliest sort of thing even if there is a silly law. I just wanted you to know, Sylvia, that I'll keep my door closed if there's this law says I have to; but it's never going to be locked, and I want all the neighbors to know the latchstring's always out and, if I'm away or something and it is locked, the key will always be here under the doormat, so you're to come in any time you take a fancy to. You'll always be welcome."

Mrs. Lodge stared at her. "That's very kind of you, I'm sure," she faltered.

"Just neighborly, nothing else. Just neighborly. After all, if folks start shutting themselves away from folks, where will any of us be?"

Mrs. Lodge didn't even try to answer that. "I'm glad you like your apartment," she babbled, as she worked at unlocking her door. "I hope you'll be very happy here."

Harriet was waiting. She knew what was the least she had a right to expect. It was bad enough she had to make the first move. A stranger moves into a neighborhood and friendly people are over immediately, introducing themselves and bringing those little things you can have to eat while you're still not unpacked enough to start your own cooking. Folks make you feel welcome. They don't wait for you to come and find them or introduce yourself or anything like that.

So this was New York and New York was different; but folks are folks the world over and she wasn't so much the yokel that she didn't know it when a woman was being stiff and unfriendly. Mrs. Lodge wasn't even pretending she kept her door unlocked and, although Harriet waited quite long enough for her to speak, she was saying nothing about where Harriet could find the keys to the Lodge door. She wasn't asking Harriet to come across the hall to visit. Obviously the latchstring was never out.

By the time the door was unlocked and Mrs. Lodge was opening it, Harriet's warm and friendly smile had frosted over.

"Well, good-by now," Mrs. Lodge mumbled, scuttling into her apartment and shutting and locking her door after her.

Harriet waited a moment in her doorway looking at the door she felt had been shut in her face. Heretofore she had been amused by the peepholes in all the doors. She had investigated her own and had been vastly entertained by the one-way glass which, when she opened its brass cover, allowed her to see out but only reflected back her own face when she tried to see in.

Now she looked at the glint of the similar glass in the door across the hall and it did not amuse her. She could well imagine that stuck-up Sylvia Lodge watching her through it right now. If people were going to be like that, she could well imagine their wanting those crazy things in their doors.

Keeping themselves all locked away and peeking out at a neighbor while deciding whether to let her in or not! What a horrid way to live! Would anyone ever want to live that way, anyone but some horrid, stuck-up snob? Convinced by now that Sylvia Lodge was behind the glass peephole watching her, Harriet vented her feelings by sticking her tongue out at the closed door and then going back into her own place and slamming her door behind her as hard as she could make it slam.

She'd left the television on and now she threw herself

into a chair opposite the set and looked at it blindly, trying to blink the tears away from her eyes.

"I don't care," she told herself fiercely. "I don't need
her. I don't care."

There was a commercial on and she'd seen it hundreds
of times before, but now she concentrated on it, telling
herself it was the most interesting thing she'd ever seen
and asking herself why she'd never paid much attention
to it before.

When the doorbell rang, it made her jump. She switched
off the TV and went to the door. She already had her hand
on the doorknob when she remembered the peephole. She
opened the metal shield and peered through the glass. It
was a man on her doorstep. She couldn't see him very well
because there was a lot of light coming from behind him
and he was little more than a silhouette. For only a moment she wondered about the light. The halls weren't
dark, but they weren't that brightly lighted. Then she
knew. The light was from the apartment across the hall.
Sylvia Lodge had her door open.

Leaving the door, Harriet went to the bathroom to wash
her face. She wasn't opening her door to any of those people, not just after her eyes had been watering that way
and they could even think she'd been crying, maybe even
crying about them.

The bell rang a second time while she was in the bathroom, but she was still undecided about answering it. She
took her time. After she'd washed her face, she fixed it. A
half hour earlier the voice wouldn't have startled her. Now
it was the last thing she expected. It would be the man
she'd seen through the peephole.

"Hello," he called. "Hello, Mrs. Langdon. You home,
Mrs. Langdon?"

She came out of the bathroom. He'd opened the door

only far enough to stick his head around the edge of it.

"Hello," she said warily.

He opened the door and stood in the doorway. Behind him she could see the opposite door also standing open with her neighbor waiting there.

"I'm Bill Lodge," the man said. "You know. We live across the hall. You've met my wife."

"I introduced myself," Harriet said stiffly. She wasn't giving an inch.

"Yes. She told me. I was wondering is Mr. Langdon in."

"No. He isn't."

"Too bad. I thought we could all get acquainted. You expecting him soon?"

"He's out of town. He won't be here till tomorrow. Tomorrow night. I expect him tomorrow night."

"Oh." Standing irresolute, he cast a despairing look over his shoulder at his wife.

She came forward. "You certainly don't want to sit here all alone," she said. "Come over to our place."

Harriet wasn't going to jump at it. "I was just about to start fixing my dinner," she said.

Sylvia Lodge came all the way. Brushing past her husband, she took Harriet by the arm. "To eat alone?" she said. "Leave it. You're coming over to eat with us."

Harriet protested that they weren't to trouble about her, but the Lodges were working together now and each one had her by an arm. They swept her out to the hall. There Bill shut her door for her. He started to release the buttons that held back the locks but paused to ask Harriet if she had her keys.

"Oh, leave it," Harriet said airily. "Let's leave both doors open and then we can see or hear if anyone comes, not that I'm expecting anyone."

The Lodges exchanged a glance. "That's not a good idea," Bill said.

"You mean we have to worry about that fire thing?"

"Unfortunately, we do have to worry."

"Then just shut them. It doesn't say they have to be locked."

"They have to be locked, Mrs. Langdon. Please, believe us, they have to be locked."

"Burglars? We don't have any of those things people steal—jewelry, mink."

"That's a good TV."

"People steal TVs? They come in and they carry a great big, heavy thing like that away?"

"It's been done."

She shook her head. "All right," she said. "Lock them if you think so. I'm sure I'll never get used to it. I'm going to hate it."

"You have your keys?"

"I have them."

She watched while he secured her door to his satisfaction. Then, when they'd gone into the Lodge apartment, she watched while he saw to the locking of his own door. She said nothing but her lips were quivering. If these people decided to be friendly, she wasn't going to stand there and laugh at them, but she'd never seen anything more ridiculous. It wasn't just the two locks. There was a bolt as well with a chain on it and he was careful to check the locks and he pushed home the bolt and attached the chain, too. Also, it wasn't just Mr. Lodge who had these notions. Everything stopped while he was locking and bolting that door.

Careful as he was, he could still have not been careful enough to satisfy his wife. She watched his every move with the locks and the bolt. Harriet had the thought that the idiotic woman was watching her husband as though her life depended on it.

XI

An hour later Harriet Langdon was in the basement, pouring at Les Gilman the full weight of her fright and shock and horror. She just wanted him to know he could start showing the apartment. She wasn't staying in the place one more minute and she was never coming back. Mr. Langdon would be around to move their stuff out or it could just stay up there and rot. Nothing would ever bring her near the place again.

Les played it cautiously, feeling his way.

"What happened, Mrs. Langdon? What's gone wrong? Isn't there maybe something I can do? What's the matter?"

"Lying's the matter," she screamed at him. "Cheating's the matter. You people think you've been so smart getting Mr. Langdon to sign that lease of yours. Well, we'll see what that lease is worth. You'll see what you can do with your lease."

Les shrugged. "If you won't tell me what's wrong," he said.

"Burglars," she shrilled hysterically. "Doors closed because it's a law in case of fire. Who did you think you were kidding? Burglars."

Les was still trying to understand it, and it still seemed dangerously tricky. He spoke only because he had to say something. He'd been thinking this moment would come, or if not this moment, one more or less like it, and he'd figured out what he'd have to say when it did come. He didn't like any of it, but he'd worked out for himself the words and the approach he hoped would be safest for him.

"Lady," he protested, "I had to tell you something."

"Why not the truth? Leaving me up there with the door not even locked."

"I've been watching. Nobody's been in or out of the building that I didn't know. If any stranger had come in or if I saw him, I would have been right on his back. If he came anywhere near your door, I would have been right on top of him. You think I've been feeling good about you up there without the door even locked?"

"I can't imagine what you've been feeling," she snapped. "I can't imagine why you couldn't tell me right out the first time you saw me. I can't imagine why you didn't tell Mr. Langdon when you showed him the apartment."

"I told him, lady. I told him the whole thing. I don't know which one he was, which of them men I showed it to, but there wasn't a one of them went away from here not knowing all about it. How it happened with Miss Wilson and how it happened with Mrs. Burns and how he's back now hanging around here every night because he's got friends on the cops and even though they had him dead to rights, they just left him go."

"Who?"

"The one they arrested for it. That fighter, the only one he had a key to the new lock. They caught him with the key in his pocket after he said all along he never had it, and they let him get away with it."

"You couldn't have told Mr. Langdon any of that. He couldn't possibly have known."

"There wasn't a man looked at the apartment, he didn't know all of it."

"You stand there and try to tell me my husband knew all about it, all about those women and everything, and he let me come here all by myself and him knowing I wouldn't even be locking the door?"

Now there was outrage along with the fright and shock and horror.

Les did his best to be noncommittal. The dame's husband must have taken just this course she was finding so outrageous. He knew that only he had been showing the apartment and he knew he'd let no man who'd seen it go away without knowing the full story. Knowing all he did, however, he was still finding it difficult to imagine any man doing what this woman's husband appeared to have done, sending her into that apartment without even a word of warning or caution when he knew all along what dangerous door-and-lock habits she had.

"I don't know," he said. "I figured he must have told you, but I've been worried about you ever since the first time I saw you because the way you acted it was like you didn't know the first thing about it. I didn't know should I tell you or shouldn't I? If your husband told you, maybe you didn't want to be talking about it, but you did know. It ain't a nice thing to be talking about, after all. Then the other way, if your husband didn't tell you, is it my business? I can't see how it would be he wouldn't want you to know, but is it really my business if you know what I mean?"

He tried hard to convey the picture of himself as a man of great delicacy, a man with the deepest respect for the sacred relationship between husband and wife. He would think many times before he intruded even one word of caution or advice.

Harriet Langdon wasn't buying it. He, in cahoots with the landlord, had tried to pull a fast one on her husband. She knew all about such things. It was no more than people had to expect when they came to New York. You could ask anyone, all over the country, everyone knew it.

It wasn't that New Yorkers were any smarter than anyone else. It was just they thought they were so much smarter. Somebody comes from the Midwest, or any other place outside this precious New York for that matter, and immediately people around here thought they could put anything over, no matter how raw. Well, they had another think coming. She was going to show them, she and her husband.

With mixed feelings Les watched her go. She was a nice little woman. She could have been an easy sort of tenant and pleasant to have around. The odds were all against his getting another he'd like as well, but still it was probably all to the good. These hysterics of hers seemed genuine enough, but there was still something funny about the whole deal.

Maybe both of them would have needed watching and maybe just the husband, but either way he was well rid of that pair. The one thing Les Gilman didn't need was any kind of tricky setup in that house. Everything had to be clear-cut and easily understood, without any unfathomable depths and without any hidden facets.

So Les played it straight. He couldn't have been more correct. He went up to the apartment, and letting himself in with his keys, he tended to the things that Harriet Langdon in the haste of her flight neglected. Where she left windows raised, he lowered them and locked them. Where she left a light on, he turned it off. He checked the burners on the kitchen range and he checked the water taps. Everything was in good order when he locked up the apartment. Everything was turned off properly.

In the morning he telephoned the office with a dead pan report of what happened. He was told to sit tight and do nothing.

"Who showed this Langdon guy the place?" he asked.

"You did."

"I didn't show it to no guy he didn't know about the murders. Every guy I showed it to brought the murders up, and he wanted so many concessions you'd have been paying him to live there. Every last one of them, they kept talking about it, about how with two murders in the place it ought to be going for practically nothing."

"He knew. He knew all about them. That's what he got the place for—practically nothing."

Les laughed. "He thought he'd get away without telling her," he said.

"That's his headache. We've got the month's rent and two months' security. They're not back in there the end of the month, we'll start showing it again. He's not getting his two months' security back. He wanted a bargain and he got a bargain. He has no beef."

Langdon surprised all of them. He didn't want anything back. He made no move to break his lease. He never made even the first attempt at pretending there'd been anything about the apartment that had been kept from his knowledge.

When his wife took flight from the place she went to a hotel, and from there she telephoned him to tell him where she was and to fill him in on how well she'd handled what had been, after all, an impossible situation.

"The nerve of them," she said. "Trying to put a thing like that over on you. The nerve of them letting me move in and letting me sit there without even a locked door."

"It's a nice apartment," he said.

"Just what I need the most, nice surroundings to get killed in."

He chuckled. "You get raped first," he said. "I thought you squaws always wanted nice surroundings for that."

She was still too close to it for laughing any of it off. "It's nothing to joke about," she snapped.

"What else is there to do about it?" he snapped back. "When are you going to start growing up, Hattie Langdon? You're no kid any more. You're no girl in the first,

beautiful bloom of her youth. Who the hell is going to
want to rape you at your age?"

"One of the women was a lot older than me and the
other one wasn't so young either. She wasn't much
younger than me if she was any younger."

"She was also a drunkard who liked her boy friends
young and rough and strong. She picked up with this tough
kid in the street. You planning on starting to act like that,
Hattie? That what you wanted to come to New York for?"

"You know all about it?"

"Of course, I know all about it. How do you suppose
we got the place so cheap? How do you suppose I got you
a New York place at a rent we can afford?"

"I don't want it. I won't live there, not for anything."

"And we won't argue about it, not on the long distance
anyway. What is this all of a sudden? We're made of
dough? You say you're at a hotel. What hotel?"

She named it and he moaned piteously. "We *are* made
of dough," he wailed. "New York with hundreds of hotels
and at least half of them cheaper than that one. You
couldn't go to one of the cheaper ones?"

"Tell me what hotel, Con. I'll move over."

"Stay where you are," he snarled. "Don't make things
any worse. I'll be there tomorrow and I'll move you out."

"Home, Con? We'll go back home?"

"You just said you wouldn't live there for anything."

"Not there," she screamed. "Back home to Ohio."

"You're crazy, but at long-distance charges I don't have
to listen. We'll talk tomorrow."

He hung up on her.

The next day at the hotel they had a stormy session.
This New York move had never been his idea. He'd known
from the first it was crazy. It was something they could
never afford. How many times had he told her just that?
How long had she been nagging him for it?

She would like to have told him that this wasn't what she'd been nagging him for, not a place where she could sit and wait to be murdered; but she'd had more than enough time for turning over in her mind all the possible arguments and she'd given up on this one.

It was no use going into that. She was past that. She was past wanting anything in New York. More than that, she was past wanting anything anywhere. What she wanted now was to wipe out of her life this whole move, to go back to Ohio and pretend she'd never been away, to have things again as though none of this had happened, to go back to feeling safe again.

"Con, darling," she babbled. "Listen to me, darling. I know all that. You're right. You're perfectly right. You told me I wouldn't like it here. You told me New York wasn't for me. I did nag you. I didn't know when I was well off. I'm sorry, Con. I'm sorry, darling. I've learned my lesson. Next time I'll listen to you. I was wrong. This isn't for me. I don't belong here. Take me home, Con, and I promise I'll never nag for anything again."

"Home to Ohio?"

"Yes, Con. Please."

"Easy as that?"

"We'll find a place there. I don't care if it isn't as nice as what we had. I don't care what it's like. I'll be satisfied with anything just as long as it's back home where I'm safe."

"Do you know what it cost me moving here? Where you planning on finding me the money for moving back now?"

"I'll do without things. I'll economize. I'll save it up and give it back to you."

He got up and walked away from her. "Nothing doing," he said. "You wanted New York. I brought you here. Now you're stuck with it."

"Not with that place. I'll sleep in the street. I won't go back there."

"Don't be more of a fool than you've got to be."

"Go over there and look at it. Go see the people across the hall. It's not only me. Look at the way people live there, hiding behind locked doors, peeking at people through holes before they dare open the door even."

"Go anywhere in this town," he answered. "It's the same. That's New York. That's how people live in this town. This is what you wanted."

Standing at the window of the hotel room and looking out, he was speaking with his back to her. She went to him and with her hands on his shoulders, she turned him to face her.

"Look at me, Con," she whispered. "I'm going to ask you something and I want you looking at me when you answer me."

"I'm looking at you."

"Do you want to get rid of me, Con? Do you want that much to get rid of me?"

He laughed in her face. "Why do you want me looking at you when I answer that one?" he asked. "You think if I'm not looking at you, I'll forget how funny it is."

"On the phone last night," she said, "you thought it was funny. I told you one of those poor women was a lot older than I am."

"And both those women were so stupid you wonder how they ever stayed alive at all. You're stupid, too, I know, but I'll draw you pictures. I'll tell you exactly what you are to do and what you are not to do and you'll be as safe as churches."

"Over there? In that awful place?"

"It's the best place we ever had to live in. It's a very good apartment. For the money it's costing us it's one hell of a good apartment. Now get this through your head.

After what I spent moving us here, there just isn't the dough for us to do anything but stay right where we are now, and that's where we're going to be. All you've got to do is remember what I'm going to tell you and you'll have nothing to worry about."

"I'll always worry."

"You'll have nothing to worry about. All you've got to do is live like everybody else lives. You keep the door locked. You don't open to anybody you don't know. You never unlock at all without first looking through the peephole. Tell me. You do that and how does anybody get in?"

"They didn't let anybody in. Their doors were locked. They even had special locks."

"They even had special locks," he repeated after her. "So you know about the special locks. Really how dumb can you get?"

"They had the same kind of lock that is now on the door, that extra one, exactly the same as is on the door now and there isn't any other kind you can get, not if you want a good one. That's the best kind there is and it's what they had, the both of them. If the best didn't keep them safe . . ."

"You do what I tell you. You'll be safe. Keep the locks on always. Never open without looking through the peephole. Never open to anybody you don't know. That's all you got to remember except for just one thing more, and that's maybe the most important thing. Don't let anybody go putting on any new locks for you. Don't buy any new locks. Don't get any locks changed."

Feeling that she was being shaken loose from her prepared defenses, she made a feeble stab at fighting a rearguard action. "If I'm going to live there," she said, "I don't want to have the same kind of lock they had, even if it is the best. Best for what? That's what I want to know."

With an air of exaggerated patience he set himself to

explain it to her. "Look," he said. "No lock is any good against a person who holds the key to it. That first dame, she wasn't smart. For that matter, neither one of them was smart. In a way what they both got wasn't anything more than they were looking for. That's the one thing you need to remember. If you don't want it to happen to you, don't go looking for it."

She didn't understand, but that happened not infrequently when he was trying to explain something to her. Mostly, however, he would be talking about things that didn't seem important. She could let them pass with a pretense that she did understand him. This she couldn't let pass. She had to tell him she didn't understand even though it meant braving his contempt and exasperation.

"Nobody goes looking to be killed," she wailed. "I don't know what you're talking about."

"Listen, stupid," he snarled. "Don't try to think. You just listen. I do the thinking for both of us."

Carefully reducing it to the simplest terms, he explained it to her. Both women were killed immediately after they had their locks changed. Nobody tampered with the lock either time. There was no evidence of any other means of entry either time. Both times the killer came in simply by unlocking the door.

"And both times," he said, putting sharp emphasis on each word, "he came just when there was only the one person in the whole world who rightfully should have been having a key to the lock and that was the woman herself."

He explained that at first, with only one killing to go on, there'd been a variety of things that could have happened.

"It could have been she had the lock put on and right off she gave somebody a key and that somebody killed her."

"Raped and killed," Mrs. Langdon sobbed. "A woman

doesn't give a man a key to her place and then get raped and killed by that man. She doesn't give a key to a man she doesn't want; and if she wants him, how can it be rape?"

He smiled at her fondly. "Sometimes, Hattie, you're too dumb to understand anything," he said indulgently, "but this time it isn't dumb. It's you're too innocent, and that's okay with me. You just stay that way. It's one of the reasons we've got nothing to worry about. You're not looking to do any sleeping around and, as long as you're not looking to do that, we're all right. You see, you start sleeping around and you never know. You can always happen on the wrong man. He looks all right. He sounds all right. A woman thinks she's going to like him fine, but when it comes right down to it, she doesn't like him at all. She can't stand him. She tells him so. She tries to push him off, but that's too late." He broke off abruptly. "Anyhow we don't have to bother about that," he said. "It looked possible that way at the first, but once the second woman got it, too, that way was out."

"How did it happen, Con? You said if it was that way, it couldn't happen to me, and now you say it wasn't that way, but you did say it couldn't happen to me."

"That's right. One dame has her lock changed and right afterward she gives somebody a key and he's a very wrong somebody and she gets raped and killed. It can happen. Then a second dame has her lock changed and right away she gets raped and killed and that changes everything because it can't happen that way twice. In fact, there's only one way it could happen twice."

"How? How did it happen?"

"They didn't give anybody the key. They had the locks changed, and the man who changed the locks for them, he kept a key and that's how he got in."

"That's how? Then how could they know?"

"If the first one didn't know, she was stupid. By the

time it came up with the second one, if she didn't know, she was crazy."

"Know what?"

"Some man you don't know from Adam comes along and he gives you a song-and-dance about how the lock you got on your door isn't any good and he's a locksmith and he works cheap and he'll put a good lock on for you right off. If you've got any sense, you know that's no way to get yourself a locksmith. You want something like that done, you go around to your local hardware store. Then, if there's anything wrong with the job, you know where you can find the guy and complain."

"A man who just goes around and doesn't have a store to pay rent on, he'll do it cheaper."

"Cheaper than what if it's something you don't need done at all? That's what I mean when I say they were asking for it. This guy rings the doorbell. He has this offer he makes for putting in a new lock. He smiles nice. He slings a good line. He's cute maybe. Sexy you can be sure he is. Nobody's going to take him on because she needs a new lock. She takes him on because she likes him and likes having him around. She was asking for it."

"But the second woman? She knew it happened to the one before right after she had the lock put on. Maybe the first one should have known, but the second one had to know. It couldn't have been like that."

"Couldn't it? You heard so much. Didn't you hear about what that second babe was. She was a drunkard and she was a whore. Didn't anybody tell you that?"

"They said she drank. They said she was having an affair with a prize fighter."

"And she met him because he was hanging around when she was moving in and he picked her up in the street right out in front of the house. Did they tell you this fighter had a key to the new lock? They found it in his pocket. He said he didn't know how it got there and he got away with it, but what do you think?"

"What can anyone think? They saw each other right along. It wasn't like you said she thought she'd like him but then she didn't and it was too late. They'd been seeing each other right along. Why would he be raping her all of a sudden and killing her?"

"He didn't. They arrested him for it and they let him go. The police aren't stupid. They know what they're doing. Sometimes they just can't find anybody at all for a crime. They can't even get started. That isn't their fault. It's like that sometimes, if a criminal is smart enough and maybe lucky enough. But if they do get somebody for a crime and they let him go, you can be sure he didn't do it. They're not stupid. When they have a man right in their hands, they don't let him go, not unless he's innocent."

"But you said . . ." she began.

"I know what I said. I said she was a whore who would take up with anybody, and mostly she was so drunk she didn't know what she was doing either. She's moving into a place where a dame was raped and murdered. You move in there and you're too scared to stay even with the doors locked. Is she scared? She's such a whore and she's so drunk and she's so crazy, she isn't even scared to pick up this young tough in the street out front and bring him up to the apartment. He keeps locking her door. He keeps talking to her about keeping it locked. She keeps saying she don't want it locked and she don't need it locked, so all of a sudden what does she do?"

"She gets raped and killed."

By now Harriet Langdon was so thoroughly confused that she'd lost track of her main concern. Now she was only trying to come up with the right answer to win back the approval of her Con.

He grinned at her. "That yes," he said, "but something

else first. This crazy woman who never locked her door and kept saying she doesn't need locks now all of a sudden changes her mind and has a new lock put on. Why?"

"You said she changed her mind."

"I meant she had it changed for her. It's that locksmith again. He comes around. He tells her it's no good having a lock the other dame had and some crazy rapist around town has the key to it. He tells her she should have it changed so nobody but her will have the key to it."

"There's a lot of sense in that, Con."

"When other people kept telling her, there wasn't any sense in it; but when a stranger comes along and rings her bell and tells her, then there's a lot of sense in it. Sure, there's sense in it because he's cute and he's sexy and she's a drunken whore and she's not such a dope she doesn't know this will be the same man, the one who changed the lock for the other woman and then came back and raped her and killed her. So this crazy whore takes him on. She thinks it's going to be exciting."

"Getting murdered?" Harriet cried. "She thought it would be exciting to get murdered?"

Her husband threw his head back and laughed. "Anything for kicks?" he said. "No, not just like that. She thinks with her it will be different. The one before was an old woman, an old maid. She'd fight him off. This one thinks with her it's going to be different. She's younger. She's no old maid. She's a divorcee, but she's also a whore. She thinks it's going to be real kicks. You see, she was too drunk and too stupid to think of what it really was. This is a man who rapes not because he can't get it any other way. He rapes because that's the way he likes it, and he kills for the same reason. Those are his kicks. Understand?"

She was trying to understand. "Yes," she said hesitantly, "but what says he won't come back, Con? What says he won't want me, too? What says he won't want to kill me, too? I'm afraid, Con."

"Nothing says he won't, Hattie, but everything says he can't. All you need is the least little bit of sense. Actually, if he does turn up, you could trap him just as easy. He tells you that you need your lock changed. You listen to his sales pitch. You pretend you believe him. You're sold. You let him change the lock. You pay him. He gives you the keys and he goes away. You go straight to the phone and call the police. It's a cinch. They fill the apartment with cops. When he comes back, they've got him. It could be as easy as that."

All the time he was sketching it in, her eyes never left his face. He could see the look of wild panic grow in them and he could see how she was trembling.

"I couldn't," she sobbed. "I'd be too scared. I could never fool him. He'd know. I'd faint."

"Yeah," Con Langdon sneered. "You'd faint. You'd just better keep it simple. You look through the peephole and don't ever let anyone in."

By the time he took her back to the apartment, she was going gratefully. Her Connie was such a good, kind man. He was so considerate of her. He wasn't insisting that, when the killer would turn up, she had to trap him. He was letting her off even trying to do it though it could have been so easy if she weren't such a coward.

XII

From his basement window Les Gilman saw them come up the street. He recognized Langdon immediately. Since he had a sharp, clear memory of every word he'd exchanged with this man, Les knew at once that this would be at least as tricky as he feared. He was going to have to watch himself with this pair. They were up to something. He didn't know what, but it was something.

He got himself up to the ground-floor hall and he was there to greet them when they came into the building. He was braced to make a bold grab at the situation.

"Hello," he said. "I didn't expect to see either of you again."

Mrs. Langdon blushed. Langdon grinned.

"Ladies!" he said. "The Mrs. tells me she got a little hysterical. We're forgetting the whole thing."

"I'm sorry I said all that stuff," Mrs. Langdon faltered. "I should never have talked to you that way."

"If I was you," Les told her, "I'd feel just the same. I wouldn't want to live up there, not for a minute I wouldn't, not if I was a woman."

He was speaking to Mrs. Langdon, but his eyes were on her husband. The man was the one who needed sounding out.

Langdon just laughed at him. "An old woman in pants," he scoffed. "What are *you* scared of?"

Les stood his ground. "I been through it twice," he said. "Twice going up there and finding women dead like that.

I don't want to be doing it no third time. Why did you think I told you all that stuff about a high rent and how they weren't going to do nothing and all like that?"

Langdon looked him squarely in the eye. "I wondered about it," he said. "When I checked with the office, there wasn't any of it true. You know, man, you were risking your job. If I told them any of the stuff you handed me, you'd be out on the street in a minute."

"Sure," Les told him. "Sure. I know and it's okay. You see, I'm not sure I want this job anyhow. People like you come along, nice people. Right at first sight I like you. I think to myself a nice man, he's going to have a nice little wife. What the hell! I don't want this job so much I can't maybe do them a good turn, maybe talk them off that apartment. It's no place for nice people like them. It's no place for anybody, for that matter."

"It's the best buy in New York," Langdon said with evident self-satisfaction. "For any town at all it would be a good buy."

"Not for you, mister, it ain't," Les insisted. "Not for a man like you, away on business a lot, not always home nights with your wife. It's too dangerous."

He could see he was making no headway with Langdon but he was having an effect on the man's wife. It was obvious. She was trying to hold it off, but hysteria wasn't so far away that the right word or two wouldn't bring it back. Les knew the right words and he was ready to use them, but Langdon had words of his own and Langdon got them in first.

For Les Gilman's benefit he went through the whole argument again, that oh-so-logical picture of the itinerant locksmith who was so cute and so sexy that the silly dames had him change locks that never needed changing at all just so they could have him around. He explained how any woman could live in that apartment in the most perfect safety. All it took was that she shouldn't be a silly idiot. He went on to tell how any woman could lay a fool-proof trap for this monster. All it would take would be a little bit of sense and the least little bit of guts.

It worked as well the second time as it had the first. In eager self-abasement Harriet Langdon apologized for her lack of guts. Les left it with assuring her that she was a brave little woman. Con Langdon laughed at the two of them. The Langdons were back and it looked as though they were back to stay. Les didn't like it. He didn't want them in the house, but he'd done everything he could think of and nothing had worked. Now he had to lie low till he managed to think of something else.

Les did try to believe Langdon might be right about him, that he had become a timid, old woman, taking fright at shadows, imagining a menace that didn't exist. Why couldn't the man be nothing more than he seemed to be, a tightwad so happy about his cheap rent that he had no trouble persuading himself that putting his wife in the apartment involved no risk. His argument, after all, was good enough to persuade Mrs. Langdon and actually it was her risk. It didn't persuade Les, but that meant nothing. Les and Langdon weren't the same thing at all. It could have persuaded Langdon.

"He could be believing it," Les kept telling himself. "He could be believing it, easy."

Given enough time, Les might have convinced himself. To believe in Con Langdon, the passionate bargain hunter, was not too difficult. Les was having no trouble with that. What stopped Les cold was the rest of it— Con Langdon, the big-hearted, generous, understanding character who went around to the office and signed the lease for the apartment and through the whole process of negotiating never once dropped even the slightest hint of the sabotage job Les had been trying to put over on the project of getting a tenant into that all but unrentable apartment.

"It didn't make him mad or anything," Les kept thinking. "It ain't natural not getting mad when somebody does you the way I done him. It ain't at all natural."

But they were back and Les had to live with it. Langdon was never out of his mind for long and, with much thinking about him, Les even began to see something natural in the man's behavior.

"He's got me where he wants me," Les told himself. "Right from the start he's done me a favor and all the time he's got that he can hold over me. All he's got to do is tell them at the office and I'm out on my ass. So far he ain't been asking for nothing special, but wait and see. It'll come. He's not keeping his yap shut for nothing."

This relatively unmenacing estimate of the situation was the nearest Les managed to come to reconciling himself to having the Langdons in the house, and even that didn't last long. Hardly a week after Langdon brought his wife back and reinstalled her in the apartment, the man went off on the first of those business trips that were to keep him out of the city for periods of three or four nights at a time. Harriet Langdon came down to tell Les her husband was gone and that she was to be alone for a few nights.

"You'll be okay, Mrs. Langdon," Les told her. "You just do like Mr. Langdon says. You don't let nobody come along and mess around with the lock you've got on your door. You just got to remember that. You'll be okay."

"Yes, I know, Les. I know, but I've been thinking I could have one of those bolts with the chain on it, too. I could have that along with the lock. You know, like other people have."

"Yes, Mrs. Langdon," Les agreed. "You could have one of them."

"I was thinking you could get me one and put it on the door for me," she said timidly.

It wasn't too extraordinary a request and there was nothing about it to bother Les particularly except the timidity with which it was advanced. The woman acted as though her husband didn't have Les just where he wanted him. Les wanted to know how genuine her timidity was.

"I can do it for you easy if you want I should," he said.

She fumbled at her purse, but he told her he'd get the bolt and chain and he'd let her know what he put out for it. She could pay him when he put it on the door.

There was going to be a little money for Les in this transaction. There was always the tip he could expect for doing one of these little extras, but in addition to the tip there was always another small sum he managed to pocket. A tenant asked him to pick up one of these pieces of hardware and to install it for her.

Les had his standard way of handling a deal like that. First of all you knew what they were charging for the thing in the local hardware store. Then you knew the big discount place uptown where they carried all varieties of bolts and locks and all stuff like that and everything cost at least a couple of bucks less than you'd pay for the things locally.

You tell them you know a place you get stuff cheaper and you charge them maybe four bits less than the local price. The odds are they add the four bits or the better part of it to your tip, but there's always the balance for sure profit.

These little opportunities didn't come Les's way as often as he liked, but Les never went to the discount place without getting a big kick out of it. His pleasure and excitement—and they came to him just from being there—far outweighed whatever joy there was in picking up his small margin of profit.

Just because it was such a big kick he lingered at the counter. It was an enormous place with swarming aisles and everywhere far more customers than the help could handle at all quickly. Nothing could be easier than lingering over a purchase. A man could be at that counter all day unless he worked up the aggressive push it took to fight past the other customers and win the salesclerk's attention.

Les wasn't throwing himself into the fight. He would eventually. He always did. There would come a time when he would notice another customer looking at him and he'd be reminded that he'd been standing at that counter a long time and that all the while he'd been showing in his face the excitement and the simple ecstasy of a kid in a toy store.

The way that other customer would be looking at him would remind him that this was an unusual way for a grown man to behave and that, if he didn't get moving pretty soon, he could even be drawing attention to himself which is what he never wanted to do when he was making one of these purchases at this particular counter.

He wasn't making any choice or decision. Obviously he wanted the solid-brass job, the most expensive one offered. That one gave him the biggest spread between discount price and list price. The little Langdon dame wasn't going to boggle at the price, and Les thought it likely she wouldn't tell her tightwad husband what it cost her. It could be significant that she waited till her old man went out of town before she even asked Les to get the thing for her.

Wiping the back of his hand across his mouth, Les was worrying about being observed and thinking it was important not to make himself conspicuous. He picked up the solid-brass bolt and chain and began elbowing his way toward a position in front of the salesclerk. Now that the

thought had come into his mind, he did feel as though he
were being watched. It didn't seem as though he had been
there so much too long, but possibly it was longer than
he thought and possibly what he'd wiped away with the
back of his hand had been easily discernible slobber.

He turned his head to look and, even before his mind
registered recognition of the familiar figure, his hand was
reacting as though with a knowledge of its own. Going
limp, it dropped the solid-brass bolt and chain to the
counter. Without even another glance behind him, he
pushed away from the counter and darted around its end
to lose himself in bathroom accessories.

Luckily the place was so big and luckily he knew it so
well. A sharp right behind a concealing shield of medicine
chests took him into refrigerators and freezers. Another
sharp right kept him clear of the lower-lying region of
ovens and ranges where a man would have to go on hands
and knees to find concealment. Kitchen cabinets offered
excellent cover all the way to the rear stairway. Les knew
there was a fire door at the foot of the stairs.

Out in the street Les had to argue himself out of breaking into a run. Bad as this was, it could still be worse. It
was still only the one man. Running would draw the attention of the whole neighborhood. He hurried to the
subway and it wasn't till he was on the train, with the
doors slammed safely behind him, that he even dared
look back.

There was nobody coming after him. As the train pulled
away from the station, he had a moment of doubt.

"Pull yourself together, man," he said. "You've begun
seeing things."

He told himself that Langdon wasn't even in the city.
Les had himself seen the man leave, complete with attaché
case and traveling bag. On ordinary days it was just the
attaché case. Les had noticed the bag even before Harriet

Langdon told him her husband had gone off on one of his business trips.

"What's to say he isn't in the city?" Les asked himself. "He goes out with a suitcase and it don't say he needs that suitcase for anything except maybe for me to see it. She tells me he's off on a business trip? Sure, she tells me and she also asks me I should get her one of them bolts with the chain to it. If they want to know where I go when I want locks and like that . . . ?"

Every fear, every suspicion he'd ever had was alive again. It was Langdon who'd been watching him at that lock counter and there could be only the one way for the man to have been there. They'd cooked it up between them, the two of them. She sucked Les into giving himself away. He waited and, when Les went uptown, he followed.

"Now what?" Les asked himself. "I got to have the bolt and chain for her. I buy it in the neighborhood and I soak her the neighborhood price. The hell with making anything on it."

Even while he was working out this answer, though, he knew it wasn't going to do. It wasn't in the neighborhood hardware store Langdon saw Les slobbering at the lock counter. It was in the cut-rate place uptown. That was bad. Les should never have let himself get caught in anything like that, particularly when he had those people spotted from the first and he knew they were laying a trap for him.

To have been seen there at all was bad, but to have been seen there when he had no reasonable explanation of what he was doing there—that would be infinitely worse. His having been there had to be explained, and no explanation could be too innocent to suit Les's needs.

There was the truth. Obviously nothing could be more innocent or safer than the truth. He'd been there to buy for Mrs. Langdon the solid-brass bolt and chain she asked him to put on the door of her apartment. But he hadn't bought it. He had it in his hand and in his panic he let it slip through his fingers, and he came away without it.

Go back for it? That was the last thing he wanted to do. He cast a stealthy glance up and down the subway car. He hoped Langdon hadn't followed him into the subway. He was certain the man wasn't in the car, but could he be sure Langdon wasn't in the next car, watching Les from there?

For that matter, could Les be sure it was only the two of them, Langdon and his wife, who'd been setting the trap for him? They could have partners all over the place, hundreds of partners, thousands. This whole subway car could be full of their partners, all of them working with the Langdons.

He had to have that bolt and chain, and if he couldn't go back for it, he was stuck with his first thought. He would buy it near home. He would go to the local hardware store for it. He didn't have to say he bought it there. He could pretend he did pick it up at the discount place. He'd have to pretend just that because otherwise how explain having been there? He would have to buy it at the list price and let her have it at the discount price.

The whole deal had turned itself inside out. It was going to cost him just the sum he'd figured as his extra profit. Not willingly or without bitterness did he prepare himself for parting with that couple of dollars, but by the time he was out of the subway he was obsessively convinced that his one hope of safety lay in spending the money.

He might have remembered that he was in no way committed to buy for Mrs. Langdon the most expensive solid-brass job. A less impressive model made of cheaper metal would carry less spread between the discount price and the list price and it would leave him less out of pocket, but he never for a moment allowed himself to entertain the idea.

Once he decided his safety depended on his doing it this way, then to his way of thinking the money it would cost him became something like a forfeit he was paying to luck or to fate or to whatever power it was he was hoping would stay with him and keep him safe even from the Langdons. Abruptly this cost took on a positive virtue. The bigger the hole it put in Les Gilman's pocket, the stronger the magic it would be for keeping him safe.

He bought the chain-bolt and took it right upstairs to attach it to the Langdon door. Harriet Langdon, already a lonely woman behind her locks, hovered over him as he worked, watching him with mixed feelings. If there was any extra protection she could have, she did want it.

At the same time she was sharply aware of the price she'd pay for her safety. She was barricading herself as her neighbors were barricaded. She was bolting herself away from all possibility of easy neighborliness. She kept telling herself she was sacrificing nothing. The neighborliness wasn't there in any case. Briefly, she'd hoped she might find it. The way the man came over from across the hall the first evening had been encouraging, but she knew now it was nothing.

What she'd been doing was too obviously dangerous. The man did his duty by her. Now they were back behind their locks and their bolt, and she was never going to get to know them any better.

So she had nothing to consider but her own safety. Watching the bolt go on, however, she was smitten with the full realization of how lonely her new way of life would be. This was more than merely giving up on the people across the hall. This was giving up on everyone. It was relinquishing all hope of a friendly passer-by. Anyone passing the other side of her door would be the enemy.

It was a chilling thought and Harriet tried to shake it off.

For as long as he was working at putting the chain-bolt up for her, she had Les in the apartment. He was, after all, company of sorts. Pulling herself together, Harriet with cheerful determination set about making the most of even this visitor. She asked him if he would like a cold beer out of the refrigerator. Chattering away, she hung over him all the time he was working.

He declined the beer and he tried to work up such an absorption in the job as would make it seem natural for him to give only scant attention to her talk. When she paused and it seemed as though some answer might be required of him, he managed to ejaculate some muffled and noncommittal monosyllable.

"Get the damn thing on to her door," he kept telling himself the while, "and get the hell out of here. Don't let her suck you into anything."

Then he was finished and all set to leave. If she thought to test out the bolt and chain while he was packing up his tools, she put it off for later. It wasn't until he was actually on the way out the door, that she came up with it and then she asked him to wait while she checked on how the thing worked.

It worked simply enough. How complicated can a bolt and chain be? Harriet Langdon, however, made a great display of clumsiness in handling it. Les had to show her how, and she made him stand by while over and over she slid the bolt to and then pulled it back again, hooked the chain and unhooked it. She was practicing.

When he finally did get himself out of there, he was in a sweat and his hands were trembling. He stopped for a moment outside the door to wipe his face and to run his hands down the seams of his pants, trying to get the palms of them dry. He heard the bolt slide home and he heard the brass chain jangle as she hooked that in place as well.

All the chores he normally had to do around the building were still to be done and he tried to busy himself
with them. He wasn't good for anything. Somehow he
couldn't keep his hands dry enough to hold a tool. Whatever he picked up dropped out of his hands. He was un-
steady.

He did only the dead minimum. What he could leave for
another day he did leave. He could think of only one possible cure for the way he was, but he tried to keep that out
of his mind until he'd done enough of the work around
the building so he could pull out without causing comment.

He had little faith in what he was about to attempt. It
had never given him all that he seemed to need, but there
had been a time when he had managed to make do with
what he could buy from a street woman. On occasions he
had been forced to make extra payment in compensation
for some unnecessary roughness, but he had managed. He
had held himself in control, only dreaming of the larger
satisfactions but firmly denying himself his ultimate need.
Killing was too dangerous. It was far more than he could
get away with. He had to deny himself that.

Even rape was too dangerous. To inflict on a woman
who had been willing even such small excess of brutality
as it took to make her switch over to resisting him had
been to skirt the outermost edges of safety. That much
risk he had always taken. It had been the nearest he could
come to the first part of what he needed, the sensation of
taking a woman by force. Whatever his further need, he
had known better than to move beyond that. Even when
in his daydreaming there had come to him the idea about
the lock and he found that, once the idea had occurred to
him, he could no longer handle the dreams and hold

them firmly in place, he had tried to pull away from the compulsion.

He'd bought the lock but even while he had been telling himself that the lock made everything possible, he'd still had the feeling that it would be too close to home to be safe. He'd put the lock away and, taking himself across the river, he'd made his try in the Brooklyn streets—out of his home territory with women he didn't know.

He'd forgotten nothing of that evening, not the kids who poured out of the drugstore to drive him off with their thrown bricks and their hoots of malicious laughter, not the woman who with terrifying competence walked him straight to the policeman. If he hadn't had those failures in the streets that night, he would never have used the lock; but he had failed and then it had been inevitable.

And it had worked. It had even worked twice. He could tell himself that even with a tenant who might have seemed right it would probably not have worked a third time, but with a tenant who'd have seemed right he would have certainly tried it the third time. More than that, he was telling himself that, as his need would have grown in him again and again, he would have tried to repeat the lock trick again and again. His compulsion would have carried him along and there would have been no stopping until the trick would have worked no longer and he would have been caught.

He tried to tell himself he was a lucky man. The Langdons were going to be his salvation. From the first he had guessed they were not the right tenant and now he knew it with complete certainty, but even that was working out for him. She had wanted the bolt on her door; and, installing the bolt, he had made himself safe from her. A bolted door made his lock trick useless. If he had needed teaching, the Langdons had taught him that a device which had twice proved safe could never be safe again.

He'd had what he'd had, but now it was over and he had to forget it. He had to go back to making do, buying what was offered for sale and pushing for what little more he could safely manage.

He took himself across the river to Brooklyn again but not to the streets where failure had forced him back home to Emily Wilson. That night he had prowled areas he had not previously known because that night he had been out to attempt an act he had previously only dreamed. Now he was going back, reverting to the way he'd been before he ever thought of the lock trick and even back of that to the street where he'd had his beginnings.

He had been very young then and in the Navy. In those days there had been the Brooklyn Navy Yard, and Sands Street that led down to the Yard gate had been the sailors' street. There the women had worn satin all the time, and as they moved, the satin, pulled tight over breast and buttock, belly and hip, gave back the light at the crest of each swelling curve.

Even back there at the beginning the Sands Street women hadn't liked his ways, but he had been Navy and along Sands Street Navy had been king. A girl could complain to her pimp, but not even the toughest of the Sands Street pimps was going to go up against a sailor. A sailor has buddies and no man is going to risk bringing the whole Navy down on him to kick his head in. That can be bad for business and bad for a man's health.

Once he had come to the end of his Navy hitch, however, he soon learned that Sands Street was no longer his territory. Sands Street women and their pimps no longer had to tolerate him. He was a civilian and alone. He could be handled and he could be driven off. He had gone to other streets in other parts of the city, but he had come away each time with the feeling that always he was risking more and having less.

Once the idea of the lock trick came to him, he couldn't force out of his mind the thought that now for the first time the whole of what he wanted had become possible for him. He didn't yield to the compulsion easily. He shied away from it. It frightened him, but he couldn't rid himself of it. He could only make the try at taking his compulsion away from his home territory.

So that night he had made his attempt in the streets and he knew better than to try that again. There was nothing for it but to reach back to the past, for a return to those times when he had done not too badly with the street women. He had still to learn that there could be no going back, that when a man thinks he has found a way into the past, he is actually backing into the future with the result a man must expect when he's not looking where he's going.

He found Sands Street changed. In the years since he had last been there the Navy had shut down the Yard. It was, therefore, less a Navy street than it had been, but most of the amenities that had been drawn to the neighborhood because of the men in the Yard were still there and the sailors who remembered them from the times when they had been stationed at the Yard still came back to Sands Street because it was the part of the city they had known and it was the area where they were most certain of finding what they wanted.

The big difference was that now they didn't come there in uniform as they had in his day. If it hadn't been for the uniformed Shore Patrol you saw up and down the street, you could hardly have known there were sailors about. The women were there as they had been in the old days and Les walked along, looking at them, trying to make a choice of which he would follow. As long as they were unaware of his scrutiny, he found it easy to delude himself that he could want one of them. The moment, however, that any of the women began to take notice of him, as soon as her eyes swiveled to him and started that lingering glide down the length of him, he sheered away.

He would tell himself that she wasn't the one, but it was obvious none of them could be the one. He kept telling himself it was because they were all for sale and he didn't want that kind.

"I wouldn't want it from the like of them," he mumbled to himself. "I don't want it when it's peddled in the street."

He hadn't totally forgotten that he chose this street because he knew it was a place where it was peddled. He did remember that he came in desperation, came because he was convinced that he was in the greatest danger and that his one hope for safety might be to go where it was readily for sale. His only chance was that he would cure himself by buying it.

He knew what he was going to have to do, but he was putting off doing it.

"Not that one," he told himself. "No, not that other one either. There's no hurry. There are so many of them, all the way up and down the street. I can wait. There'll be one I'll like better, one I want more; and even if there isn't, I can always settle for one of these. For one of these there's plenty of time. These'll be around right on down, always around, walking the streets and peddling it. I don't want it from them even if they was giving it away."

He tried to think of it as just a way of speaking, but underneath, in the part of himself he was refusing to look at or think about, he knew it was the simple truth. He didn't want it if they were giving it away. What was given was no good to him. It had to be what he took, and by violence. Then there was the one thing more it had to be, the last act for which somehow he would find a reason to make it seem as though it had nothing to do with anything that went before.

A blonde in green satin came across the street toward him. There was a lot of heavy, black fringe ornamenting the satin. The fringe looked so much like monstrously enlarged mascaraed eyelashes that all up and down her, wherever one of her curves undulated outward, her body seemed to be winking at him. Transfixed more by astonishment than by interest, Les forgot himself and stopped to stare at this phenomenally draped blonde.

The blonde, who didn't trouble herself with distinctions between interest and invitation, mistook astonishment for approach. She attached herself to Les's arm.

"Lover boy," she crooned, "what kept you so long?"

He tried to pull away from her, but she hung on. Blind with revulsion, Les forgot everything but fighting free of her. He had to get himself out of her hands. He had to get away. He struck out at her with his free hand. Taking the blow full in her face, she let go of his arm and staggered backward.

A big young fellow came up behind her and caught her. With fluid, athletic ease, as though he were executing some thoroughly practiced team maneuver in an intricately organized game, he passed the now-blubbering, green-satin bundle into the hands of a slightly smaller pal and, on the follow-through, neatly pivoted into Les.

His first punch dropped Les to the sidewalk where immediately Les was encircled, the center of a quick flurry of kicks. Les knew what this was—the Navy banded together against the civilian, the outsider. He shot his arms up to protect his head.

"They'll kick my brains out," he was telling himself.

He didn't bring his arms down until the two giants with the SP armbands had him hauled to his feet. By then the blonde in the black-fringed, green satin had disappeared and, out of all the big boys up and down the street, Les couldn't even make a guess at which one knocked him down or which of the others closed around him to kick him where he lay.

The SPs wanted to know what happened, but Les had nothing to tell them. The whole thing had gone wrong. The whole thing was a mistake. The quicker he got off the streets the better. The idea that brought him there to save himself had slipped away from him. Now he wanted to run home. He was falling back on the instinct that told him he would be safe there. For the moment he forgot that there he would be most unsafe because there he would be confronted by the Langdons and the trap they'd set for him.

Mumbling to himself, he started away. He was limping a little with the pain from a line of bruises along his thigh, but worse than that was a pain in his side. It stabbed him with every breath he took. By keeping his hand pressed tight against his ribs and keeping his breathing as shallow as possible, he managed.

As he went along the street now, he was only dimly aware of people. He had a blurred impression of kids and women. He seemed to be walking between walls of them, and the walls drew back, edging away from him as he approached, and they came together again in the wake of his passing.

He was aware of the two shore patrolmen where they followed along behind him, but he wasn't thinking of them as what they were, his guarantees of safe passage. He had them lumped with the kids who poured out of the drugstore after he ran by and with the patrolman who watched so sharply when Les jumped the bus.

A man could always be all right if there weren't all these people to interfere. Interfering, watching, following, driving a man away from anything that could be easy for him or right for him, hunting him along the streets, harrying him into traps.

The SPs saw him out of the neighborhood, not leaving him until he'd gone for a couple of blocks through streets where there was nobody but themselves and Les. He walked on alone, but all the time the pain in his side grew worse. He came into some streets that were dark and deserted and completely quiet. When he reached about the midpoint of a long row of boarded-up houses, he stopped and lowered himself to the steps of one of them to sit there a while and take stock of his hurts. The stone of the steps was painful for his bruised thighs, but the bad pain, the one in his ribs, eased off a little while he was sitting quietly.

He had been a considerable time resting on those steps when he heard the woman come down the street toward him. The shuffling sound of her walking told him nothing. That could have been either a man or a woman; but, on and off, she broke into snatches of song, and her voice, however husky, was still unmistakably a woman's.

Except for shifting his hand to find the tape he carried in his pocket, he didn't move. He was making a deal with himself. He was giving himself no choice. He wasn't going to move. He was going to sit right there and do nothing. More than that, he was going to go on doing nothing unless it came to him. That was it. It had to come to him because that way he'd know it was something that had to happen, not anything that happened because he wanted it that way, not anything that happened because he made it happen. He was putting the whole thing away from his own hands or his own volition. It would be only if it had to be.

The woman could turn around and go back the way she'd been coming. She could turn off at the intersection that still lay between them. She could cross the street and pass on the other side. She could go into one of the houses she would reach before she came to the one where Les sat waiting on the steps. She could even stop at one of the other boarded-up houses and settle herself on the steps to rest there the way Les was resting. She had all the choices in the world and Les was making no moves. If she came to him it would be only because that was the way it had to be.

The woman came straight on toward him, singing her snatches of song, shuffling along the pavement. Even when she was no more than a few feet away from him, Les didn't move. He just moaned. The woman stopped and peered toward the steps. He could make her out as little more than a shape. It was too dark to tell whether she was young or old, good looking or ugly, neat or slovenly.

"You drunk?" she asked. "You drunk or you sick?"

"I'm hurt," Les answered. "I'm hurt bad."

She came closer and bent over him. Her breath made his head swim.

"Where are you hurt?" she asked, finding his cheek and ear with her fingers and fumbling at them.

Les reached up and took a firm grip on her arm.

"Here," he whispered. "Here. I'll show you."

He flipped her against him so that he had her pinned tight between his arm and his side. His free hand brought the tape out of his pocket. In the morning her body was found; but it wasn't until someone, concerned for decency, pulled down the clothes that had been hauled up over her head, that they could see how her lips had been sealed with the tape or how the killer's hands had come down on her throat.

The men who found her had known her alive. They were neighborhood people and for a long time she'd been a familiar, neighborhood sight. She was an old woman who had her monthly Social Security check. She had fixed herself a place to sleep in one of the boarded-up houses, and there had been speculation on how long an old woman could live on liquor alone. So far as anyone knew, she never ate.

Nobody expected she would live long, but nobody ever dreamed she would die as she did. Nobody could imagine what sort of a man it could be who'd have wanted her at all, much less wanted her enough to take her as she was taken and to follow it up by strangling her to death.

XIII

Inevitably the police connected the Brooklyn rape-murder of the elderly derelict, Rose Eaton, with Manhattan's Wilson and Burns cases. Rose Eaton, like the two earlier victims, was a woman who'd ordinarily have been rated as conspicuously not rape-prone. Like Emily Wilson she was notably lacking in the physical attractions expected to inflame a man. Like Claire Burns she was so extraordinarily accessible that it hardly seemed necessary under any circumstances for a man to use force.

More than by these broad similarities, however, the police were impressed with similarities in detail. The taping of the women's lips was the telling bit. Post mortem examination showed that in all three cases the tape had been slapped on to the women's mouths. In all three cases such savage force was used in the application of the tape as in itself amounted to an act of violence.

It was the same brand of tape, the same width, and the same grade as was used on Wilson and Burns. Even on superficial examination the police had that much. Out of their labs came more. Microscopic examination of the three pieces of tape showed up an otherwise invisible irregularity of weave, a bias thread of slightly greater thickness and weight. This thread occurred in all three pieces, and piece to piece its ends matched up perfectly to draw its oblique line across the width of the tape.

Tape from the one roll had been used successively to seal the lips of the three women. From the night of Emily

Wilson's murder right through to Rose Eaton tape from that roll hadn't been used for any other purpose. Between murders the roll of tape lay fallow. The three pieces in the hands of the police were three consecutive segments ripped off a single, continuous strip.

Even the simplest cop could read that. All three killings were the work of one single rapist-killer. Nothing was different in the Rose Eaton case except the shift in the scene of his operations, and that difference readily explained itself. The two previous tenants of the Twelfth Street, Manhattan, apartment were women who lived alone. The new tenant was not a lone woman. This killer played it safe. He went after none but lone women.

Routine procedures followed their routines. The pair of detectives who dropped in on Bob Herman when he briefly had the dishwashing job and who ever since at frequent intervals came by to remind him that he wasn't forgotten, went around to Grady's and picked Bob up.

They came so early that they had to rouse him to let them in. He was there alone, sleeping on his cot in the storeroom. If they were jumping to conclusions, so was he. They were a long time getting to the place where they were talking about the same thing. They wanted to know where he'd been that night.

"Around," he said.

"Where around?"

"Just around."

"Around Manhattan?"

"Yeah. Where else?"

"Where else?" they repeated after him. "Around Brooklyn maybe. That's where else."

"Brooklyn," Bob said, thinking hard. "Last time I was in Brooklyn was two, maybe three, years back. It was in Greenpoint. I had a club fight over in Greenpoint."

"Not Greenpoint. Like near where the Navy Yard used to be."

"I don't even know where the Navy Yard used to be."

"I bet you don't."

"When was it? When am I supposed to have been over there?"

"Tonight. Between one and three tonight."

"In Brooklyn?"

"You heard us."

"Tonight between one and three you know where I was."

"That's right. We know. We just want you to tell us."

They'd backed him through the empty saloon to the room where he slept and where he kept his things. While they questioned him, they went through his stuff. The police had been through his stuff before this and he knew about it. It was the time they took him out of Claire's apartment. They went through his pockets then, both of the leather jacket and of the shirt and pants he had on him. He was told that later they went to his room and went through all his stuff there.

So now it started in the same way. They checked the pockets of the pants he pulled on when he went to let them in. Then they turned to the clothes he wore that night, stuff he'd taken off and had lying around the room. At first, when they were just going through pockets, it wasn't much different from the way they went through the leather jacket that time at Claire's; but then later it was completely different.

If they did look at his stuff that way the first time, he wasn't there to see them do it and that made all the difference. It wasn't as though they were looking for anything in particular. It was rather as though they were examining his clothes inside and out to determine whether or not he kept himself clean. Nothing like this had ever happened to him before. It made him hot with shame.

"You got a full report on where I was," he growled.

"That's right," they said blandly. "We just want to have it all over again from you, boy."

There was no reason for not telling them. He'd been walking. The whole neighborhood knew how much he walked. Now that he wasn't going to the gym and doing any regular training, he walked all the time. It wasn't like roadwork; but for now, when he wasn't doing any regular training, it did help with keeping his legs in shape.

Walking, as he did, not to go anywhere but just for the exercise, it didn't make all that much difference where a man walked. So they couldn't expect him to tell them exactly where he'd walked or he could pretend they couldn't because even what he did remember of it he preferred not to say.

Even if he gave it to them only by the street names, they would recognize the polarity of his walking—the place where Claire used to live, the gym where he used to train. They would recognize the way he had to keep himself away from people, going to Grady's only after lock-up time after Grady was rid of the night's last customer.

There was no reason for trying to keep any of this from them. He was convinced there was nothing of it they didn't already know. They kept telling him as much and the only reason he could imagine for their wanting it from him was to force him into the humiliation of the recital. In exactly the same way he could see no reason for their messing around with his clothes that way, as though they were trying to learn whether he'd been peeing his pants. It could only be to humiliate him and he wasn't going to play along. He didn't have to give them that. Nobody could make him.

"Ask your man," he growled. "Don't go asking me."

It was crazy from the first and abruptly it went crazier.

Messing around in his things, they came on his roll of tape. He couldn't understand why they picked on that rather than on his other things. It was just part of the stuff Grady picked up for him from his old manager. Bob would have said it was the most trifling and least important thing he owned.

"Where'd you get this?"

Bob had been through enough questioning to recognize the tone. One of them comes up with the tape. He shows it to the other one. They're elaborately dead pan about it, but he can sense their excitement. Then they start with the questions about it and they put on their most elaborately casual tone. He remembered an earlier time when the performance was just about identical. They acted this way when they found Claire's key in the pocket of his leather jacket.

"I always had it," he told them.

"We went through your room last time. You didn't have it then."

"I had it."

"Don't lie to us."

"Who's lying?"

"Anything you had then we saw. You didn't have any tape. We went through every last thing you had on you and every last thing you had in your room."

"I had a locker. Over to the gym I had a locker."

"Without a key? We went through everything in your room and you didn't have any locker key. All you had was the keys you had on you, two keys—the one to your room and the one to the dead babe's new lock."

"The lockers over to the gym, there ain't no keys to them lockers."

"What kind of lockers have no keys to them?"

"The kind over to the gym, the kind with the combination locks on them. No keys. The tape wasn't in my room like my jock wasn't and my ring shoes wasn't or my sweat socks or my trunks. Why don't you go smelling around them?"

"We're asking you about the tape. When did you use the tape last?"

"Last time my hands was taped. I don't remember when that was. It's been a long time."

"What else do you use it for?"

"Nothing. You go in the ring, you tape your hands. You don't tape nothing else."

"Out of the ring?"

"Nothing. I don't use no tape outside of the ring."

"You wish you didn't," they told him.

They took him downtown. They also took his roll of tape. The tape disappointed them. It was the wrong brand and the wrong width. It did them no good.

They shoved him into the line-up and that also did them no good. Their opposite numbers across the river in Brooklyn were hard at work. Casting a wide net around the street where Rose Eaton died, they combed the area for people who might have noticed a man behave peculiarly.

Since their questions dealt with only one specific variety of peculiar behavior, they didn't catch up with the woman on Sands Street or with the sailors who rallied to her or the Shore Patrol. That man who'd been seen on Sands Street had behaved peculiarly enough; but when busy detectives were hunting a rapist-killer, who would trouble them with that drip? He had behaved as though he were afraid he might himself be raped.

The Brooklyn detectives did, however, find people who had seen a peculiar looking man. In the wake of any act of violence there will always be people who saw a man. Their descriptions of the man they saw are likely to be as various as are the witnesses themselves, but none of the descriptions bore much resemblance to Bob Herman, and when they came to the line-up and saw Bob, nobody picked him as the man they'd seen.

After that it was more of the same, different teams of detectives taking turns at questioning Bob. In every respect it seemed to be the mixture as before, threat alternating with cajolery, threat and cajolery coming together in all possible blendings. If the tape had been right, they could have pinned him down with that. If in the face of his denial of having been in Brooklyn even one witness had recognized him, that also could have helped them.

With nothing working out in either of those directions, they were back to the old, familiar position. Bob Herman hadn't been cleared. They just didn't have as much evidence as would be needed to do anything about him.

The one thing that was most different was that Bob this time was not relying on just the simple denial. This time he kept insisting that he had an alibi and a witness for it. This time there was nothing lost from memory, no blank interval, no period of alcoholic fog. This time he was telling them where he'd been all night and, more than that, he insisted that, if they would, they could find a witness to back him up.

His trouble was it was a witness he couldn't produce. He expected the police to produce the man for him. He didn't know who the man was or where he could go to find him, but he was certain the police knew. The man, he kept insisting was one of them. He couldn't understand why they didn't go to this man and ask him. He also couldn't understand why the man wasn't coming forward to tell them.

"It was about half past twelve I first noticed him," he said. "He was tailing me and he went right on tailing me down till I went home. That was long after three and it was all in the neighborhood, never more than twenty blocks any direction away from Grady's, no place even near Brooklyn."

"This man, this detective, you say. Had you ever seen him before? Had you ever noticed he was tailing you before?"

"Never before, but that night and all the time that night."

"For hours you walked the street and he tailed you and all the time you knew he was there. You didn't talk to him? You didn't ask him what he wanted with you?"

"I knew what he wanted with me."

"What? What was that?"

"He had his eye on me. Like you're always telling me. You all got your eye on me."

"But you didn't ask him. You didn't even know he was a detective."

"Who else spends his nights like that?"

"Not nights. Just the one night. You never saw him except the one night. That's what you said, isn't it?"

"That's right."

"And you expect us to believe that? This man is never around except the one night and for just the time when you need him. You don't know who he is except you tell us he's a detective, and how is he a detective when we don't know about him? You expect us to believe a story like that?"

They didn't believe it, but when they tried to hold him, the DA's office again wanted no part of him. The DA's men conceded that Bob Herman's alibi was as near to useless as any alibi could be. A man would have to be pretty stupid to offer an alibi like that, but how stupid would the DA have to be to go after an indictment against a man when all you could prove on him was stupidity?

XIV

Behind her carefully secured locks and with her bolt driven home, Harriet Langdon slept well. When shortly after three-thirty that first night she had the bolt on the door the keys slid stealthily into first one of her locks and then the other and then, with the locks opened, the door was pushed against the brass bolt, Harriet heard nothing. Even when the door was shaken and it rattled against the bolt, it wasn't enough to wake her. It might have been because it was done only most gently and softly, but it might also have been because, feeling safe and secure, she was having so sound a sleep.

She slept straight through the whole of that aborted invasion, and when she went to her door the next morning she found it exactly as she left it the night before. Both locks were secure. The bolt was well seated in its socket.

She had only this one night of sleeping that well. The next evening her husband came home. He was patient with her and kind, but he was also firm. His Harriet was a womanly woman and that was all right with him. He couldn't have loved her half as much if she hadn't been. He wasn't an unreasonable man. He wouldn't be angry with his wife just because she wasn't what he wanted her not to be—one of those forbidding creatures with the mind of a man, capable of sensible, logical thought.

"You're an idiot," he said. "You know you're an idiot, my dear."

"Why, Con? What have I done now, Con?"

"That silly thing you put on the door. What's that for?"

"The bolt? It's the safest thing. They have one like it across the hall."

"It's fashionable," he said, taking on a tone of gentle raillery. "I'm lucky they didn't shave their heads and paint their skulls black. I could be coming home to a wife who'd be looking like an 8-ball."

"It makes me feel so much safer, Con."

"It doesn't make me feel safer. It scares the pants off me."

"It's only a bolt and there's the chain you can put on when the bolt's off. That's for opening the door so you can hear what somebody wants and still keep him out. It isn't anything to be scared of."

Gently and patiently he lectured her on the hazards. For anyone to shut himself up alone behind a bolted door was the most dangerous stupidity. He ran through a catalogue of disasters: legs broken in bathtub falls, fires, gas leaks, coronaries, strokes, hemorrhages.

With the locks she'd already had on the door it would take only the simplest common sense for her to keep out of the apartment anyone she didn't want coming in. The bolt was unnecessary and dangerous. Alone behind a bolted door, if she suffered even a minor accident, it could grow into a fatal disaster before help could reach her.

"If you're such an idiot," he said, "that you'd unlock the door and let some strange man in, why does the bolt make you smarter? You're just as likely to unbolt the door to let him in. Then what do you think would happen?"

"Please," she begged. "Please, Con, I don't want to think about it. It scares me to think about it."

"If you're going to be silly," he said, affectionately drawing her toward him, "I must make you think about it. Think of how I feel. I have to be away from you so much of the time. Think of how it'll be for me if I can't be sure you're safe."

"You just tell me what to do, Con."

He told her. The bolt should never have gone on the door, but it was there. Now it couldn't be removed without having the door repainted and they couldn't afford to have that done. Therefore the bolt would have to remain on the door, but he was trusting her to use it only in the very special circumstances he would outline for her.

She was never to bolt the door at any time when she was alone in the apartment. She was never to have the door even on the chain at any time when she was alone in the apartment. If he was there with her, that was different. That, however, was hardly worth talking about since she'd need neither bolt nor chain when he was home.

The only use of the chain she was to permit herself would be to put it on when she was answering the door. The chain could be put on immediately before she opened the door to talk to someone. It was to be taken off immediately after she had the door shut and locked again.

The bolt she was permitted to use even more rarely. It would be only in that most unlikely event that a man came to the door and he would be a man of whom she didn't like the look. In that case, if she inspected him through the peephole or spoke with him around the edge of the door she'd been keeping on the chain and she had then shut and locked the door against him, and if then he didn't go away but started working on the locks, in those circumstances and only then would it be permissible for her to ram the bolt home.

"It's no good for anything but that," he told her. "Only to help keep him out while you're picking up the phone and calling the police. You understand?"

She understood, and he went downstairs to speak with Les Gilman. By the time he'd finished with Les, there was hardly a soul in the building who hadn't been made thoroughly conversant with Con Langdon's thinking about bolted doors and with the strength and violence of Mr. Langdon's feelings on the subject.

With Les he was neither gentle nor patient. He accused the man of talking Mrs. Langdon into having the bolt and chain just so he could make himself a little money out of installing the thing for her. For the first time he harked back to the day he came to look at the apartment and he said that, starting way back then, Les had been consistently working on a scare campaign. He reminded Les of the word or two he might have dropped at the office. He cautioned Les that he could still drop that word or two. If Les didn't want trouble, he'd better begin minding his Ps and Qs.

Les wanted no trouble. With mounting fear he was watching trouble close in around him. There was the vicious pain that seared his ribs with every breath he took. He knew he should have been to a doctor about that pain, but he didn't dare go. Doctors asked questions and this much Les knew. He had to avoid questions at all costs even if it meant making such efforts as he could at doctoring himself.

If before Con Langdon came downstairs to make his loud and angry scene over the chain-bolt Les Gilman felt he was caught in a steadily rising trouble-tide, now he knew there would be no ebbing of that tide until the troubles swept over him and he was drowned in them.

Ever since he'd put it on the door, Les's one last shred of hope had been that bolt. Behind that door lay his last, big trouble, but he would be all right. Somehow he would be all right because there would always be that bolt to stand between him and the final disaster.

Now the man was giving him ruddy hell for installing the bolt. He was shouting that the bolt would never be in use. He was asking Les what kind of an idiot he was not to realize that Mrs. Langdon's safety depended on the constant possibility that, whenever necessary, Les should be able to reach her, simply by going in with his duplicate keys.

"Whenever necessary."

The words kept repeating themselves in Les's head, and Les knew about necessity. There was only the one little chance left to him now. He was going to have to run. It wasn't the first time the idea had come to him. He'd thought of it before and rejected it. It would be too long before he could get away, far too long for living within reach of that Langdon trap.

He could think of no way he could go about shortening the time. He would quit the job. He'd been thinking about that possibility ever since the day Langdon brought his Harriet back to the apartment. Even then he'd been wondering whether Langdon could be what he seemed, and he'd been certain the man was up to something.

Now he was telling himself he shouldn't have waited around to see how things would come out. He should have given his notice at once or better still he should have begun at once hunting another job. It would be no good running away from that trap upstairs unless he could take all the time he'd need to make it look perfectly innocent, perfectly natural, and like anything in the world but flight.

A man goes hunting. He finds himself a better job. It's got better hours, more pay, better working conditions, fringe benefits—anything at all to make it clearly enough better to make it seem natural that a man should change jobs. When a man's found himself such a better job, he can give notice and nobody will wonder why.

The quick getaway would mean taking no time for finding another job. It would mean just up and out without giving notice. Then everybody wonders why, and Les Gilman is in no shape for having anybody wonder about him.

Actually, he'd never done more than think about it. He'd never even begun the job-hunting preliminaries. There was one most important thing a new job would have to have in addition to whatever it would be that would make it look like a job worth moving to. It would have to be some line of work totally different from these apartment house jobs he'd always had. It would have to be something where he wouldn't have keys to anyone's apartment, where he would not in any way have access to any women. Les had thought the thing through that far. Just changing over to another job could in itself be a trap.

Two dames in this building during the time Les was working there. Then after Les makes the move to a new job, a dame over there? What would even the dumbest cop make of that?

A job where there would be no women? Where can a man like Les Gilman go to find a job like that and, if he did find one, wouldn't he be changing from a job where he was an experienced hand to one where he was completely without experience? And still the new job would have to be clearly better than the old one.

A job where there would be no women? What kind of a job could that be? Les was without ideas. He did have the one thought that he might enlist, but he knew that for any of the armed services he'd have to take a physical examination. A man who had to treat himself because he couldn't risk the questions a doctor would ask was certainly not hazarding any physical examinations, even if he weren't fairly sure he was over the age they'd be taking.

A man had to be in shape before they'd take him. They wouldn't have any part of a man who'd just about given up breathing because it hurt him so much every time he drew a breath.

There was no place for him to go, and now he knew he couldn't stay where he was. He compromised. He went around to the office and he gave them their two weeks' notice. It would have been better if he could have explained to them that he was leaving to take up a more attractive offer but he was afraid to chance a lie.

They did ask him why he was leaving and he answered with the almost-truth that seemed to him safest. He was too nervous to stay. Twice already murder had happened over his head and he wasn't staying around to have it happen again. With the apartment vacant, he'd been all right. With a couple going in there he'd been all right. He'd promised himself though that if it ever happened again that there would be a woman alone up there, he was going to quit.

They protested that the Langdons were a couple. She wasn't this woman alone he was talking about.

"He's a salesman," Les answered. "He travels. He's away on business more nights than he's home. More nights than not she's up there alone. I've had enough of that. I didn't want them taking the place. I did everything I could to stop them taking it. There oughtn't be anyone living there at all and mostly not a dame she's there alone at night."

A building superintendent who tells the agents right out that he's done everything in his power to keep a hard-to-rent apartment unrented becomes an employee they can expect to be better without. They accepted his notice and began looking around for his replacement.

So then it was only two weeks he had to worry through and with the pain in his ribs, which day after day grew no better, he kept telling himself he wasn't up to much. He was a sick man. It was no more possible now than it had been before for him to report himself sick. He'd given his notice and he could have lain down and not done another lick of work on the job. What could the building owners have done about him? They could have fired him out of there before the term of his notice was up and he would have liked nothing better, but he had to keep his eye on the ball.

He had to remember that right on through, everything had to seem completely natural, completely innocent, and completely right. He'd always done his work conscientiously and now wasn't the time to make any changes in that. The important thing was to remain inconspicuous, to do nothing to draw attention to himself. He had to stay with it. He had to sweat it out.

Only six days of his two weeks had gone by when the night came around. Only that same morning he'd seen Langdon leave with his luggage. This would be the man's first out-of-town trip since the one when he'd left in this same way only to turn up in town spying on Les at the lock counter in the discount place. He made a great point of letting Les know he was "going on an out-of-town trip again." He told Les how many nights he expected to be away. He even half jocularly warned Les against taking advantage of his absence.

"If you have any ideas of selling Mrs. Langdon any more of your nonsense hardware," Langdon told him, "forget it."

Les spent the whole day trying to forget. When night came, he went out. He tried a movie, but that was no good. Even though he carefully looked for just the seat and didn't let himself settle in until he'd found one where he was on the aisle and there was a man in the seat beside him and a man in front of him and a man behind him, it was only a short time before the man alongside him got up and left.

A woman slid into the place. As she squeezed by, her thigh brushed his legs and her perfume enveloped him.

Les hurried out of the theater. He went to a bar and

had a drink. There was a kid at the bar who was trying to impress the bartender. He was telling the barman about having been across the river to Jersey the night before. The kid told about the strippers as though they were the first the world had ever known. The bartender played him along, pretending to be the complete innocent.

"They did?" he exclaimed in counterfeit incredulity. "Stripped down barebutt? What did your girl say?"

"I didn't take my girl there," the kid yelped. "What kind of a dope do you take me for? Nobody goes taking no girls to a place like that. No dames at all in the audience. It's all men, just men."

Les tossed off his drink and went out of the bar, knowing at last where he could go to be safe for a while. He went down to the terminal and hopped a bus over to Jersey. The grind houses weren't hard to find. The one he settled into was all the kid claimed for it.

There were no women except at a safe distance. They were all on the stage or along the runway, where they belonged to another world. Although these babes of the other world troubled him, he did feel safe as long as he was confronted with them. They were beyond his reach. However disturbing they might be, they were safe and this was the one thing Les couldn't let himself forget even for a moment. His safety depended on theirs. No woman anywhere could be in jeopardy without putting Les Gilman in jeopardy with her.

He stayed in the theater till the place closed down and then he went to a neighborhood bar, but that was no good to him. A woman came up beside him and wanted him to buy her a drink. She came up from nowhere. There was no refuge. Les headed for home.

He knew it was wrong. It was the one thing he knew he must at all cost avoid, but all day he'd known that finally there would be no avoiding it. He kept trying to tell himself nothing was going to happen. He knew better than to let it happen and anyhow he was too sick. He wasn't good for anything. The pain in his side never did let up, not even for a moment.

It wasn't as though he were anywhere near being ready. Everything was wrong with it except her husband's being out of town that night, and Les was even asking himself what wasn't wrong with that.

There was the time just a week before when Langdon had also been out of town except that he hadn't been out of town for all that he kept letting out that he was. What was to say it wouldn't be the same game tonight? It would be one way the trap could be worked.

Nobody could have given him a reason or an argument he wasn't throwing at himself, but it was never any good. He kept trying to tell himself he wasn't going to do this and he wasn't going to do that, but the compulsion fastened on him by Langdon's departure that morning was moving him along.

He had no intention of going into the apartment. He was going home, to his own place in the basement, and he did. But then he couldn't settle in. He went to the box where he kept all the duplicate keys. He wasn't going to take them out of the box. He was just going to look at them. He only wanted to make certain they were still there, that they hadn't been stolen or tampered with, that they were all right.

But then they were in his pocket and he was stealing upstairs with them. He wouldn't go into the apartment. He told himself he wouldn't. He was going to show himself. This was a test of strength. That was why he had the keys with him. He could go upstairs and right past her door and he could have the keys in his pocket and he wouldn't use them.

He wasn't crazy. He wasn't falling into any trap, and

anyhow he had that pain that kept him from breathing. He was too sick. Sick as he was, there was no danger in having the keys with him.

There wasn't even any danger in his trying the door. He wasn't going to open it or go in. He was just going to try and see if it wasn't on the bolt after all.

For all her husband's shouting around about it and for all her promising her husband she wouldn't ever have it either on the bolt or the chain when she was alone in the house, Les was betting with himself that, if he took the keys out of his pocket and unlocked that door, he would find it wouldn't budge. She would have it securely bolted.

This was something Les had to know and it would be so easy for him to find out. He wouldn't open the door and he wouldn't go in. He would just assure himself that she did have it bolted and then he would feel safe again. He slid the key into the upper lock, the special one. Nothing happened. It wasn't possible. He tried it again.

This was the later part of it. This didn't come so early. It never came so early. This was for when people came looking for her and he had to show them how his keys were no good. There was no way he could get in. He knew what this meant. The lock had been changed, but when with him having no memory of it?

He was certain he hadn't been in the apartment and he was certain he hadn't changed the lock, but he was asking himself if he could be certain of anything. That crazy chance or the crazy series of chances he'd taken over in Brooklyn, that wasn't like him. It was nothing like he'd been always before when he'd always been so careful and never taken even the smallest risk. Taking risks was a crazy thing to do and once a man started going crazy could he say where he would stop? Could he say he would stop short of the place where he'd have done things and not even know he had?

In a panic he pulled his key out of the unbudging lock. He was forgetting about keeping things looking normal. He was forgetting that he still had a little more than a week to go on his notice. He was running now. He was in blind, unthinking flight.

He didn't run far. As soon as he'd turned away from the door and headed for the stairs, the door opened behind him.

XV

Bill Lodge was an early riser. He was also a jogger and he liked to take his exercise before breakfast. Every day it was straight from bed into a sweat shirt, slacks, and sneakers and out for his morning run. He always jogged the same route and on his return he always followed the same routine. His key in the lock would wake Sylvia and while he shaved and showered and dressed for the office, she would prepare their breakfast. Most mornings she woke when he did but she enjoyed dropping back for that extra interval of sleep while he was out jogging. Her return to sleep, however, always waited until after he was out the door. She lay back on the pillows but, before she would let her eyes shut, she had to hear the firm click of the door as he shut it behind him. It was the sound that told her that the lock tongues had lodged firmly in their sockets.

Bill knew that she lay listening for that sound just as he knew that when he returned and put his key in the lock, he had to get the door open quickly and, even while it was opening, he had to shout at her. It wasn't that there was any such panic rush about getting him his breakfast. It was because even the softest click of key in lock would bring her full awake and she would lie with her heart stopped until she had the reassurance of hearing his voice.

Poor Sylvia had never recovered from the shock of the Emily Wilson murder. That was when she had begun being nervous about the locks, and naturally enough, too. But little by little she had almost begun to relax and then there had been the second one, the Burns woman. After that staying on in the apartment just across the hall had seemed impossible.

They had been there a long time and it suited them. Since they had it at a controlled rent, anything else they might find was going to be far more expensive, but there had been nothing else for it but to go looking. They had been doing just that but only to find that the cost of anything else they could use was even worse than they had imagined. They were still looking, but day by day the urgency had been draining out of their search. They were not yet ready to say straight out one to the other that they might stay on in the apartment after all, since fear seemed to diminish even as you learned to live with it and they had both been happy there for so long a time, but the thought had been creeping up on both of them.

There were, therefore, manifold reasons why Bill would be most careful that the door should be locked after him. Obviously he wanted to keep Sylvia safe. Also he was a considerate man and he knew the state of Sylvia's nerves. He was more than willing to observe any ritual that might bring her even the slightest reassurance. Finally, there was that sneaking hope he had hardly begun to confront even in his private thoughts, the possibility that they might stay on and once again come to have that same enjoyment of the apartment as they'd once had. At best it seemed a slim hope. Let Sylvia be subjected to another shock, and there would be no hope at all.

Having just performed his careful ritual of checking the locks, Bill turned from the door to start trotting down the stairs. Immediately he saw the body. It was on the stairs just a few steps down from the apartment. It was the body of a man. The back of the man's head was a sickening viscosity of blood and hair, and beside the man's body lay a blood-smeared block of brass. Lodge recognized the metal thing before he had any recognition of the man. It was a lock; and, although he had only just finished checking his own lock, in his first moment of bewilderment he looked back over his shoulder to assure himself that it was where he knew it was, still solidly set in his apartment door.

Even as he was turning to look, he knew he was being absurd; but then he still had to force himself to look at the other door, the one across the hall from his own.

"Not again," he was moaning.

The sound of his own voice shocked him out of his dazed paralysis. A look at the Langdon door also helped. He saw that it was as firmly closed as his own with its locks properly in place and nothing to indicate that there might be anything wrong with it.

So it was just the man and the blood-smeared lock. On second look he recognized the man. It was the building superintendent. For a moment he groped for the man's name. Les. Leslie? Lester? He didn't know and it didn't matter.

The man was dead. Bill hadn't even for a moment thought that he could be anything less than dead, but he did stoop beside him for a closer inspection, not so much to make certain as still trying to make himself take the thing in. He touched the man's hand and recoiled from the chill of it. He started back toward his own apartment but stopped short before he had even fumbled the key out of his pocket.

He didn't want to go back inside to telephone to the police. He didn't want Sylvia to hear him come in and he didn't want her listening when he made the call. He realized, of course, that there couldn't be the slightest hope that she wouldn't have to know. There was no way she wouldn't know and once she knew they would have to get out of there. Without consciously thinking it out, how-

ever, he moved, carried along by a wish to postpone the
moment when he was going to have to confront her with
this newest shock.

Instead of doing the most natural thing, which would
have been to go back inside and use the phone in his own
apartment, he edged past the body and ran down the stairs
and out to the street. He could make the call from the
pay phone in the booth at the corner, but then he found
that he didn't even have to go that far. On his way to
the corner he ran into a policeman. In that way it came
about that the first police officer on the scene was not the
precinct detective who would have gone out in response
to a telephoned call. It was Frankie Giordano, the patrolman on the beat.

Giordano went back with him. Giordano did a more
thorough check of the body to determine that Gilman
was indeed dead. It took him only a moment, and in that
same moment he noticed what Bill Lodge hadn't seen or,
seeing, hadn't recognized for what it was.

The bloody head wound was obvious, but the marks on
the dead man's neck were hardly less obvious, and Officer
Giordano was beginning to think of himself as something
of a specialist in the field of that sort of bruise when it
appeared in that area. Just ahead of them at the top of the
stairs was the apartment door behind which he had twice
discovered the bodies of women who had died of manual
strangulation. This time it was a man and this time it
was the other side of that apartment door, but the bruises
were the same.

Giordano indicated the door. "That your place, mister?"
he asked.

"Lodge," Bill told him. "No. We're the other apartment,
the one opposite. People name of Langdon live in there
now. That's the apartment the two women had. One after
the other, they . . ."

Giordano spared him the saying of it. "Yeah," he interrupted. "I know. It's always me, seems like. Both of them, I was the one went in and found their bodies. Could I use your telephone, Mr. Lodge? I've got to call this in."

Bill squirmed. "Mrs. Lodge," he stammered. "My wife. Hearing me come back in now right after I left, a lot sooner than she's expecting me, it'll give her an awful fright. You know, living here after all that's happened, she's a bundle of nerves. We're going to have to move."

"Okay, okay." Sorry for the man, Giordano hurried to get him off the hook. He tried the bell at the Langdon door. "I'll make my call on their phone. I know how it would be about Mrs. Lodge."

He wanted to believe that he could use the Langdon telephone. He wanted to think there would be an answer to the doorbell and that it would not be as it had been twice before, but there was that bloody lock lying on the step beside the dead man's head. Giordano was not unaware of the messages that lock was putting out. He tried to think they might not mean what he thought they meant, but he could see nothing else they could mean.

Whether he would get to the Langdons' telephone or not, ringing the Langdons' doorbell would in any case be the thing he had to do first. This was his third time at this same door. He knew all the moves. He leaned on the bell and gave it enough time to make certain that he was going to have no answer there. Giving up on it, he turned back to Lodge.

"If you think you'll be all right here with the body," he said, "it'll only be a couple of minutes while I run downstairs and make my call."

Lodge meanwhile had been preparing himself for accepting what he'd thought would be coming next. Failing at the Langdons' door, the patrolman would say there was no help for it. He would have to use Lodge's phone. Pleasantly surprised by this other suggestion, Bill jumped at it.

"I'll be all right," he said. "It's my wife is the nervous wreck. I'm all right."

"You won't touch him. You won't touch anything?"

"Not on your life," Lodge said.

"A couple of minutes. That's all."

"Take any time you need. I'll be fine."

Giordano ran down the stairs. He was remembering the time he'd come in with Bob Herman and pulled Gilman out of his basement apartment to bring his keys upstairs. Gilman had gone with them that time, leaving his own door ajar and again, when they'd gone back down to the basement for the ladder, once more Gilman had come away from his own apartment without locking up after himself. If that had been the man's habit, there would be a phone Giordano could get at down there. There was also the ladder.

The door wasn't standing open this time, but when Giordano tried it, it wasn't locked. He went inside and put through his call to precinct. During the moments he was on the telephone he was also looking the place over. It seemed much as it had been when he had been there before. If there was anything different, it was not significantly different. Giordano told himself there was no reason for anything to be even suggestively different. What had happened to Les Gilman had occurred upstairs.

As he had promised Bill Lodge, he was only a few moments on the telephone; but then he didn't go straight back up the stairs to where he'd left Lodge with Les Gilman's body. The ladder was in the apartment just where it had been both the times Gilman had given Giordano the use of it.

Giordano carried it out to the yard. He knew where to go and just which was the window. Climbing the ladder, he worked on the explanations and apologies he would

need if it should turn out that the Langdons were heavy
sleepers and hadn't heard the bell. He had no expectation
that he would need apology or explanation, but it was
what he wanted to think. He could think up no alternative that he could prefer to this possible embarrassment.
As soon as he had come up to the window and looked in,
however, he had to stop thinking about anything but that
one alternative he had been certain all along he was going
to find.

Through the window he saw not two people in bed but
just one, a woman. The bedclothes were a tangle and her
nightdress was rumpled and torn and on her face where
there should have been the red of her lips he could see
instead the neat white rectangle.

"Jesus," Giordano whispered as he climbed in the
window. "Again and again and again."

He knew the woman would be dead and he knew there
would be those same bruises on her throat. He was telling
himself he didn't have to look, but he was a good cop and
he checked everything out carefully. She was dead. She
did have the bruises. Even as Giordano was telling himself that she was exactly as the other two dead women had
been, it seemed to him that there was a peculiar difference. Where the previous two had shown some little
evidences of having fought against their attacker, however
futilely, there was an odd look of repose about this one
as though in her case every last bit of the violence had
been her murderer's alone. She looked as though she had
taken what came without even a moment's effort at ward-
ing it off.

Giordano looked around the bedroom and could see
nothing that seemed significantly different. Each of the
women had had her own style—Emily Wilson's prim neatness, Claire Burns' slapdash confusion, this one's penchant
for ruffly pink trifles—but now, as both times before, the

room looked as it might well have been when its occu-
pant in the most peaceful and ordinary way had tucked
into bed.

Out in the living room he used the telephone to tell
precinct that he had a second body for them that morning.
The living room was also as he had expected it would be,
no indication that anything had been disturbed. Without
any conscious thought of what he was looking for he was
concentrating on the chairs and the sofa, doing an inven-
tory of all the places where a man might fling a jacket or a
coat or sweater or any other thing of that sort a man might
wear outdoors and pull off when he came in. There was
nothing. Recognizing what he had been looking for,
Giordano shook his head.

"He wasn't here," he muttered. "Not Herman. Bob
didn't even know this one."

The thought that Bob did know Les Gilman, that there
had been an enmity between the two men that could have
led to any bad end, and that Herman had been all too lavish
with his threats against Gilman did push itself at him, but
he didn't want to give it any headroom.

He shifted his thinking to Bill Lodge instead. He'd left
the man out in the hall with the body. He'd promised
that he'd be gone only a few minutes, and although he
hadn't been long, the time was beginning to stretch. Lodge
had assured him that it was Mrs. Lodge who had the nerves,
but Giordano hadn't failed to notice that there had been
considerable sweat and not of the kind that normally went
with the exercise outfit Lodge was wearing.

He started for the door. There was no point in leaving
the man out there with the corpse. It couldn't be doing
the poor guy's nerves any good, and the man did have a
tough time ahead of him with his wife. The hinged
brass plate that served as a cover for the door's peephole
hung open. Before touching his hand to the locks or the

doorknob, Giordano looked through the peephole. He had
a clear view of Lodge. The man looked as though he were
coming apart. He was shaking visibly. He was standing
with his back planted tight against the door to his own
apartment as though he had chosen that as the only direction from which he could be sure nothing hostile would
come at him from behind. He was darting frightened
glances in every direction, but he seemed most concentrated on the door from behind which Giordano was
watching him. Giordano couldn't tell whether the door
was merely a welcome alternative to the horror of looking
at the corpse on the stairs or whether the Langdon apartment represented the direction from which Lodge was
afraid something would jump out at him.

"He's not expecting me to come this way," Giordano
thought. "All I'd have to do is touch the locks and I'd
frighten the piss out of him before I could have the door
open and he could see it was me."

For a moment he thought of going back down the ladder
and returning to Lodge by way of the stairs; but, even as
he was thinking of it, he heard the sirens. The reinforce-
ments from precinct were arriving. He waited a few moments more and they were on the stairs and through the
peephole he could see Lodge sag with relief. He unlocked
the door and came out to talk to the detectives.

In the apartment they found two shiny keys that fitted
the shiny lock in the Langdon apartment door. In Gilman's pocket they found two keys tagged with the Langdon apartment number. One fitted the house lock in the
Langdon door. The other fitted the bloody lock that had
been used to bash Gilman's head in.

The evidence of how Gilman died was clear. The lock,
viciously swung against the back of his head, struck him
down from behind. The blow could have been lethal. It
would certainly have knocked Gilman unconscious. Not

satisfied with knocking Gilman cold, however, the killer
had completed the job by taking the unconscious man by
the throat and strangling him.

There were none of the usual signs of struggle shown
by the cadaver of a strangling victim. The killer had
come up behind Gilman and that might mean Gilman
had never seen the man at all. That was the theory
Frankie Giordano was taking up, and he didn't like it when
the detectives told him the evidence wasn't conclusive.
There were two ways it could have happened. As Giordano argued, Gilman could have been hit from behind by
a man he never saw. In that case it would follow that even
if the killer had allowed the super to remain alive, he
could have made his getaway and been safe from being
identified by Gilman. Then why kill the man?

"Look what he hit Gilman with," they said. "The old
lock. How come he would have the old lock handy? He
was in the process of putting on the new lock and he was
doing it late at night, far too late for any normal locksmith to be working. So he's an abnormal locksmith, and
what else have we been looking for? Gilman sees the man.
Immediately he knows the score. Why should he stand up
to him and be a hero? He turns to run. The killer goes
after him. So Gilman has to die. The killer is a man he
recognized. The killer is a man he can identify. This one
cinches it on your pal, Herman."

"Because he hates Gilman's guts or because Gilman can
identify him?" Giordano asked.

"For both reasons. Aren't two reasons better than one?
And there's another thing. Look at the tape on her mouth.
It's not the same width as the tape he used on the others.
It's taken from another roll. From the going over we gave
Herman on his roll of tape when we picked him up on
the Rose Eaton job, he's a cinch to know he couldn't go on
with his old roll of tape. Who else would use the tape three

times and change it the fourth time? Someone smart enough to worry about what we can do by piecing tape together? Somebody smart doesn't make the mistake of using the same tape three times. Somebody who's been tipped to it by the questioning we put him through the third time? He's the only one we questioned about tape."

Even while Patrolman Giordano and the detectives who'd responded to his call were still checking out the bodies, the locks, and the apartment, another pair of precinct plainclothesmen went around to Grady's and gathered in Bob Herman.

This time he offered not even as much alibi as that peculiar deal he'd persisted in repeating when they'd picked him up for the Rose Eaton job. He'd been to a movie. Since he said he went alone and neither the ticket taker nor the ticket seller remembered him, there was no corroboration there. After the movie he'd taken a walk. He admitted that his walk had taken him past the house, that he had even been past there many times in the course of his walk, but he denied having been inside the building. He swore again and again that he'd never been in there since the day they found Claire's body. After his walk he said he went home to Grady's. He didn't get there till after Grady locked up for the night, and Bob used his key to let himself in. So that was it. Except for the fact that he had indeed been at Grady's when the detectives went around there to pick him up, there was only his own word for it that he'd gone home at all that night. There was nothing to say how long he'd been there before the detectives came around.

His questioning, therefore, began much along the same lines as they had been over with him those previous times. The only new ingredient came from probing into the history of his feud with Les Gilman. He made no effort to deny his feelings about the man. He had only the one word for him—shithead—and he used the word freely. He asserted stoutly that he'd never let Gilman get away with anything and that he never would. He was calmly confident that he could under any circumstances at all handle Gilman.

For the most part his denials were weary and routine. He had been through so much of this too many times before. He responded mechanically. The only part of it that seemed to rouse him at all was the suggestion that he'd held the brass lock in his hand when he knocked Gilman cold. He didn't need anything in his hand if he was going to deal with that shithead. He didn't even have to throw a real punch at Gilman. A little tap knocked Gilman on his can. Bob had witnesses to that.

XVI

To the detectives Bob Herman's denials were no more convincing than they had been the other times they'd questioned him. If anything, he was less persuasive this time. When the bottom did drop out of the case they thought they were going to build against him, it was not as a result of anything Bob had found to say in his own defense.

It was solid evidence and it came from sources no precinct detective could even try to impeach: from the Medical Examiner and from the police lab. The post mortem on Harriet Langdon established that there was no discrepancy between apparent cause of death and actual cause of death. She had died of manual strangulation accomplished with great force. According to the ME's findings she had been sexually used shortly before her death and the sexual assault had been brutal.

In contrast, however, the taping of her lips had been done with incongruous gentleness. In the opinion of the ME, with that one exception of the way her mouth was taped, everything done to Harriet Langdon had been done with a violence far in excess of what might have been needed. There was nothing to indicate that she had struggled at all or that she had offered even a token resistance. Even the condition of her lips backed this finding up. They looked as though she had never so much as strained against the tape in an effort to cry out.

Similarly the examination of Gilman's body turned up no evidence of the man ever having closed with his assail-

ant to put up even the feeblest struggle in defense of
his life. His head had incurred from the heavy brass lock
damage so grave that it was certain that he had been immediately unconscious. Even if the blow had not been
followed by the strangulation which caused his death, he
would have remained unconscious for a long time. In all
likelihood, the Medical Examiner indicated, the cerebral
damage alone would have been enough to take the
man's life with little possibility that he could ever have
regained consciousness before he was dead. None of that,
of course, was news to anyone who had seen Gilman's
body when it lay on the stairs, but at that time no one
had seen him with his shirt off.

The Medical Examiner found the whole of the right side
of Gilman's chest encased in a crisscross of dirty, wrinkled
tape. It hadn't been newly applied any time just before
the man died. It had the look the stuff picks up only
when it's been there for a week or more, and under the
tape the skin showed that maceration it takes on when for
a period of many days it's been sealed away from the air.

The autopsy revealed a couple of broken ribs and torn
intercostal muscles. It was the ME's opinion that these
chest injuries had been suffered by Gilman a week or more
before his death, that they had been severely painful, and
that they would have hampered the man very considerably in his movements and activities. The taping had been
done too clumsily and ignorantly to have been of any
benefit. The injuries appeared to be the result of a savage
beating. They were so severe that ordinarily a man would
have sought medical help for them. Only a man most firmly
addicted to doctoring himself or a man with compelling
reasons for avoiding a doctor would have handled them
as Gilman did. There was, of course, no way the Medical Examiner's people could determine which it had been
in Gilman's case.

It appeared that at the time of the fatal assault on the man he had, as a result of these chest injuries for which he'd received no useful treatment, been in no shape for giving any sort of decent account of himself in a fight with even a weak opponent, and his opponent had been by no means weak.

There was also evidence that shortly before the man's death there had occurred an ejaculation of semen. Whether the ejaculation was spontaneous or in an act of sexual union could not be determined.

The police lab took up where the Medical Examiner left off. Working on the tape that had been taken from Les Gilman's chest, they reconstructed the order in which each strip of it had been applied. The outermost strip of tape—the one that would have been the last to go on—was recognizable since it was the only piece which over the whole of its nonadhesive surface was dirty and which, over the whole of that same surface, showed nowhere a trace of adhesive gum. On this evidence the lab boys knew that it had nowhere been overlaid by another strip of tape.

With that established, the rest was ridiculously easy. Under the microscope the tape showed up a flaw, a thread that was heavier than the rest and that ran its full length. Since the telltale thread didn't run parallel to the edges of the tape, by matching flaw-thread to flaw-thread, the lab boys reconstructed the whole tape all the way to the piece that had to be the first strip applied to Gilman's chest. From there it carried along in perfect continuity: The piece that had been taken from Rose Eaton's mouth, the piece taken from Claire Burns' lips, all the way back to the first piece, the one that had been used to still any outcry Emily Wilson might have made. On measurement, furthermore, they found that the individual pieces added up to a full roll. Gilman had begun a fresh roll of tape with the piece he'd slapped on Emily Wilson's mouth and had used up the last of that roll when he'd done the clumsy taping of his own chest.

The Brooklyn men who had been working the Rose Eaton killing took it from there. Checking back over the descriptions they'd had of a strange man behaving oddly in the neighborhood of her murder on the night of her death, they came on three that gave promise of fitting Gilman. Returning to those three witnesses and showing them an assortment of mug shots among which were included pictures of Les Gilman, they secured three firm identifications. Each witness in turn pounced on the Gilman pictures and each in his description of the man's odd behavior included details of peculiar movement that would have been the unavoidable result of Gilman's then newly fractured ribs.

Following up on that information, they traced him back to Sands Street where they filled out their history with the Shore Patrol account of the beating Gilman had taken there. At that point the Brooklyn detectives had everything they needed. They could close out their investigation of the Rose Eaton murder. On that side of the river all questions had been answered.

Back in the old precinct the thing worked out almost as neatly. Only one loose end remained. Everybody was agreed that the rape murders had been solved. The tape was conclusive evidence to fasten the guilt on Les Gilman. That on the last victim, Harriet Langdon, a piece of tape from another roll had been used raised no questions. The laboratory measurements accounted for every last inch of the roll that had been started with Emily Wilson. Since Gilman had finished that roll with the taping of his own chest, it was an easy assumption that he would necessarily have begun a fresh roll for the sealing of Harriet Langdon's lips. That neither on Gilman's body nor among his things down in his apartment were they able to find the roll from which that piece of tape had been taken was annoying; but, after an exhaustive though fruitless search, they fell back on a not unreasonable hypothesis. Gilman had had among his things an old roll of tape of which there had been only the short strip left. Thriftily he had used up that old remnant on Harriet Langdon instead of going out and buying a fresh roll.

Reversing the time sequences to see through the trick he had worked with the lock changes was easy. So long as they had been looking for the rapist-killer his device had kept them fooled. It had been a question of what man had access and all through the times when the door had on it locks to which Gilman held duplicate keys, Gilman had been the man with the most obvious access. By changing the lock and leaving both keys to it inside the apartment Gilman had put himself even with the rest of the world. He had no more access than anyone else. He was the man who could have just walked into the apartment at any other time. Who was going to suspect him of finding a way into it on the one night when it would be difficult, the one night when there was a lock on the door his key wouldn't open?

Once it was no longer a question, however, of who the man was but only a matter of how Gilman had worked it, the puzzle evaporated. It became obvious. He had never gone in past the new lock when he went in to rape and kill. He had gone in, as it had always been obvious that he could, while his duplicate keys would still open the locks. The lock change in each case had come after the crime, not before.

On all that everybody was satisfied. The one remaining loose end hung not from any of the rape killings but from the death of the rapist. Who killed Les Gilman?

By this time it might have been habit that had all investigating personnel handing the election unanimously to Bob Herman.

Where previously they'd been after Herman to admit that he committed this double killing and the three rape murders that went before, now they wanted him to confess that, since they'd been so wrong about him and had given him so hard a time, he had become his own detective. Somewhere along the line he'd come to suspect Gilman. All that hanging about outside the building hadn't been, as he insisted, just taking walks and a man had to walk somewhere. He'd been watching Gilman.

He caught Gilman just as the man finished changing the lock. What could be more natural than to pick up the lock that would be lying there where Gilman had set it down? It was right there ready to hand. Anybody would pick it up and let Gilman have it.

"Look, kid," they said. "You're okay. Nothing's going to happen to you. You help us. We'll sew this up, and the whole damn thing's over. You'll never have any trouble over it again. You'll be a hero. You'll be fighting again. There's nothing here to hurt you. You'll be doing yourself a lot of good."

Bob couldn't be persuaded.

"The last time I was in that house you was there, too," he said. "It was after Claire died, when we went in and found her—Shithead, Frank Giordano, and me."

"Look, kid. You don't trust us. We can understand how you don't trust us, but we're leveling with you. Actually, we've always leveled with you, haven't we?"

"I ain't been inside there ever."

XVII

H. Conover Langdon came home to bury his wife. To say that the man was beside himself with grief would be to understate it. From his very first words he gave every evidence of being all but out of his mind under the unbearable burden of his self-reproaches.

The detectives heard him out. They were sympathetic. They were patient with him while he unburdened himself. Going through the necessary formalities with the man, they made it as easy for him as they could. Since they showed him so much consideration, they left him unappeased in his appetite for self-accusation. The newspapers picked up where the police left off. The reporters encouraged him to pour everything out. They were having from him a great sob story, and he gave them all the story they could want.

Nothing was ever going to persuade him that the blame could lie anywhere but with him. He had been wrong every step of the way. He had been weak. He had been stingy. He had been too ready to please his Harriet. He had been too penny-pinching to do it the right way, letting it cost what it would.

"So I saved the dough," he said. "Now look what it's cost me. What was I saving for? Our old age? I was going to retire and we'd be together all the time. It was to have the money for that. So I saved and there'll be the money, but look what I've lost. Who's going to have this old age to spend it on? Not Harriet."

The move to New York had been made against his better judgment. They couldn't afford New York, and he'd known it. That's where he was wrong in the first place. He should have said no and nothing should ever have changed him. No matter how much she coaxed, he should have had the character to go on saying no.

It was an easy guess that once the word would have been nagged, but his Harriet was dead and he was taking all the blame on himself. He said coaxed.

"It was so we could be together more of the time," he said. "It isn't easy to go on saying no to that; and then I saw I could get this place and, with all the bad publicity it had, I could get a lease where living here was no more than it'd been costing back home in Ohio. I figured why not. Harriet wanted it so bad and I wanted it, too."

"You weren't afraid of the place, Mr. Langdon?" the reporters asked.

"I guess I talked myself into it. It would be all right. You want something enough, you talk yourself into it. God, was I being sensible. I did a whole analysis on it like it was a business proposition where you weigh the risks. I said to myself to look at the two women murdered here. The first one? The way it was with her it could happen to anybody. She had no warning. The second one? From all accounts that one was an alcoholic and a whore. What happened to her couldn't happen to my wife. If my wife was letting anybody in, she'd know who it was. Harriet never took a drink in her whole life. She was W.C.T.U., Harriet was."

"It makes a big difference," they assured him. "About the first woman, though, you were saying she had no warning. Did you, Mr. Langdon, before you moved in here tell your wife what apartment it was?"

Langdon sighed. "I know what you mean," he said. "The people across the hall and what they told her and her go-

ing to a hotel and all that. I saw you had all that in the papers. You're right. I didn't warn her. You see, gentlemen, Harriet was a timid woman. If you know how she carried on when they told her about the two earlier tenants, you'll understand what I mean. I wanted her to be happy here. Once we were making the move, I wanted her to be happy, not scared all the time."

"And you thought she could be happy and safe as well? Didn't have to be warned?"

"I told you," Langdon moaned. "Every step of the way I made every possible mistake. The whole thing right from the beginning, it's all my fault."

"Bear with us, sir." Reporters are persistent. "We don't understand. You did an analysis of the proposition. You weighed the risks. Emily Wilson, the first tenant murdered here, had no warning, but your wife was going to be all right without warning?"

"Warning or no warning she wasn't going to be safe. I know that now. We all know it now. If anybody knew it before, that lunatic would have been put out of the way and it would have been all right. The way it was then, it's this locksmith. He goes around putting on locks. He keeps a key for himself. At night he comes back, lets himself in with his key, and you know what." He winced away from the rest of it and nobody was going to press him there. "Why is it always this one apartment?" he continued. "Why no place else in the house? Isn't it because here there's been women living alone, not couples? I figure it's that way and my wife will be all right."

"Even though you're traveling a lot on business and there are many nights when she is a woman alone?"

He shook his head. "Not what I mean," he said. "Not at all what I mean. A woman lives alone, she has to make her own decisions on things like what kind of locks she has on the door and all that. My wife doesn't know the first

thing about hardware or locks or anything of that stuff.
A man comes to our door and wants to put a new lock on
it, she sends him away or at the most she has him come
back when I'm home. Nobody has to give her any warnings
about wandering locksmiths. I handle that sort of thing
in our family, and I have been warned."

He went on to say that, as things worked out, if she
hadn't learned about the murders from the neighbors, he
would have had to tell her himself. He explained that it
had never occurred to him that she wouldn't right at the
outset see that New York was different from their little
Ohio town and that she couldn't bring to the city her old
home habits of leaving doors unlocked or keys under door-
mats.

"Anyplace in New York," he said, "that wouldn't be
safe. I never thought she had to be warned off doing that,
not that it made any difference the way it's turned out."

The reporters sighed with him. "No," one of them said.
"Since it was the super, nothing could have made any
difference."

Langdon wasn't letting himself off that easy. "There was
one thing," he moaned. "The bolt. If she had the bolt on,
and it's my fault she didn't. I was so afraid she would get
sick or something or there'd be a fire and behind a
bolted door nobody could get to her. You see, I never
thought this other could have happened unless the lock
was changed first."

Patrolman Frank Giordano, shield number 954376, read
the newspapers. Every one of them carried the story of
Langdon's grief and of his bitter self-reproaches, and
Patrolman Giordano read all the stories. He read them
obsessively because inside the uniform and behind the
shield there was Frankie Giordano, and Frankie was a
troubled man.

The detectives had given up on Bob Herman. They were

no less convinced that Bob was the man who had caught
up with Les Gilman and had written *finis* to Gilman's
career of rape and murder than they had earlier been convinced that Bob Herman himself had been the rapist-
killer. Earlier, even when for want of sufficient evidence
they had been forced to turn Herman loose, they had not
given up on him. As long as the rape murders had remained
unsolved the detectives had been under pressure to make
an arrest and to back it up with evidence adequate for trial
and conviction. There had been the pressure they put on
themselves, and there had also been the pressure that
came down on them from above. That there should have
been such a series of crimes and that these crimes should
go unsolved made them look bad. It also made the department and all the law-enforcement machinery look bad.
It frightened the citizenry and it raised a public outcry.

This later situation, in which nothing remained unsolved but the death of Les Gilman, weighed on them little if at all. One could be technical about it and argue that
the killing of Les Gilman was also a crime. Any citizen
who surprises someone in the commission of a crime has
the right, if not even the duty, to make a citizen's arrest.
Like a police officer he has the right to use as much force
as is necessary for subduing the criminal and preventing
his escape. The law, however, frowns on the use of excessive force whether that force is exerted by a police officer
or by Mr. Ordinary Citizen.

Obviously using the lock to knock Gilman's head in had
constituted sufficient force. The blow had knocked the
man out. The criminal had been subdued. He could easily
have been secured. There would have been no possibility
of his escaping before the police could have come and
taken over from the public benefactor who'd brought the
mad dog down. To have grabbed the unconscious man by
the throat and choked the life out of him had certainly

been an exercise of excessive force, but then who was to care? What man could say that in a similar situation he would not have been so gripped by horror and rage that he, too, would not have been beyond any capacity for making fine distinctions between the sufficient and the excessive?

Most people, as a matter of fact, would not even concede that what had been done to Les Gilman had been at all excessive. In a state where his crimes would not have subjected him to the death penalty and where it would have been universally felt that society could never take a chance on a man so monstrous being again at large, it would be only the rare purist who would not feel that killing Les Gilman, even if it hadn't been precisely legal, had been precisely right. The community was now forever safe from the horrifying results of his mad compulsions, and the taxpayers had been saved much trouble and much money. If there was any criticism of his killing to be heard, it was only that he hadn't been castrated first.

Even if the law might require that some formal charge be brought against this public benefactor who had cleansed the community of this menace, the man could certainly suffer no penalties. He would be a hero. He would be untouchable. Nothing would be done to him. Everything would be done for him.

So Frankie Giordano read the newspapers and Frankie was troubled. He was overcome with pity for Langdon, but he was also overcome with worry about Bob Herman. Along with the worry he was further troubled by a feeling of guilt. All through the time when the boys on the detective squad had been hounding Herman, Giordano had been the suspect's friend, cleaving to the principle of innocent until proved guilty. Frankie, however, had seen the evidence against Bob Herman. He had been the one who had held Bob after the Claire Burns killing and he had been the one who had turned Bob over to the detectives.

Frankie could tell himself that he had done no more than his sworn duty. He'd had no choice. He could not, however, feel happy about the part he had played in what now was revealed to have been the unjust persecution of Bob Herman. Blameless throughout, Herman had suffered contumely, loss of livelihood, scorn, hate, and ostracism.

That troubled Frankie. More than that, though, it worried him that now, when all this should have changed, all too little was different. Herman was no longer being hounded. The precinct detectives were off his back, but apart from that, he was still much where he had been ever since Claire Burns was killed.

Frankie was a good cop. He knew his neighborhood. He knew his people. He had a sharp sense of what they were saying and thinking and feeling, and they were just not sure about Bob Herman. They had lived too long with the rumors that said Herman was guilty and that, having friends at court, he had been turned loose again and again to prey on those poor women. The rumors persisted. Even though there was no longer any police action to feed them, they spawned, seemingly of themselves, such small additions as were needed to keep them going even in the face of all revelations about Gilman.

Herman's friends had been taking care of the rat all along. Now they had all they needed to do a really good job for him. They had a dead man on whom they could fasten Bob Herman's crimes. Dead men don't talk back. Dead men can't defend themselves.

Frankie had been hearing the talk.

"I don't care what anybody says. I know."

"Where there's smoke there's fire."

"Oh, yeah? He done nothing? What was he hanging around the Burns piece for all the time?"

"And what about the way he was always hanging around that house all the time after?"

"Yeah. How about that? I seen him there myself. I never went by there I didn't see him."

"Everybody seen him."

When the detectives had given up on Bob Herman, Frankie Giordano made his try. Did Bob know what people were saying? People? Frankie could take people and shove them. But Bob owed it to himself to set everybody right. There was the whole world out there waiting to pour its gratitude on him. All he had to do was say the word. Didn't he want to fight again? Didn't he want to go back to the gym, go back to living again? The way he was, it wasn't living.

If he was such a crazy that he wouldn't think of himself, there was Grady. Grady was his friend. Grady had been good to him. Didn't he think he owed Grady anything? Wasn't Grady managing him now? Wasn't Grady running his ass down to a nub trying to get Bob a fight and nobody wanting to touch him?

"All you got to do is tell it like it was, kid," Frankie begged. "You knew the louse. The first time you was ever over there, you tangled with him. You had this hunch there was something not right about him. That's why you hung around over there as much as you did. You was watching him, and all the time you've been taking all the shit everybody's been throwing at you, you was watching him until finally you caught him. You been taking the blame long enough. What's wrong with taking the glory?"

"I ain't never been up there," Bob said. "Not since after Claire. Out in the street, but never inside."

It was all Frankie could get out of him, but Frankie couldn't leave it at that. He had an idea. Bob was never going to listen to him. Bob was a chowderhead and a mule, but it wasn't only that. It was what Frankie was as well. Frankie was a police officer, and Bob had been taking too much at the hands of the police.

"I can see how he can't trust me," Frankie told himself. "If I was him, would I trust my old buddy, Frankie Giordano, when he was the one went all over pig and no part buddy, listening to that Gilman instead of to me and starting me out on all my grief? The fuck I would."

Frankie couldn't leave it at that. He felt that it was up to him to find someone against whom Herman could have no grievance, someone Herman *would* trust, someone to whom Herman would listen. He was on his time off, but he couldn't feel that any of what he was doing was like pulling duty. It was something Officer Giordano didn't have to do. It was something Frankie Giordano was compelled to do for himself.

He went around to see H. Conover Langdon. Langdon was glad to see him. Langdon seemed eager to talk, as though he could never have enough of going over all the mistakes he had made and of pouring the blame on himself. Frankie listened patiently even though it was all a repeat on what the papers had run in their interviews with the bereaved widower, and Frankie had read all of it. He listened, waiting for a moment when he could work things around to asking Langdon if he would do what Frankie wanted of him. Langdon came around to wailing about the way he had made poor Harriet leave the door off the bolt.

"Don't go blaming yourself for that," Frankie told him. "You weighed the risks and rode along on the one with the better odds. Anyhow, since it was Gilman, the bolt wouldn't have done no good either."

"He couldn't get in if the bolt was on," Langdon insisted. "Nobody could."

"That's not it," Frankie explained. "It's who could have snowed her into opening up. Gilman comes to the door. The bolt's on. He rings. She looks at him through the peephole—when I found her body the peephole was open. Let's say she's very careful. She puts the door on the chain and opens it just the slit it'll open against the chain. Gilman talks to her. He tells her there's a leak downstairs. He has to come in and check. Why wouldn't she let him in? How could she keep him out?"

"Then there was never a chance," Langdon sobbed. "Once I made the first mistake of moving in there, we never had a chance. Nothing really mattered after that."

Giordano waited for him to pull himself together. Langdon blew his nose and wiped his eyes.

"I hate to bother you," Giordano said. "I been thinking maybe you could do me a favor."

"Anything I can do," Langdon said eagerly. "That's the worst of it. There isn't anything I can do."

"It's this fellow, Bob Herman," Frankie began.

"I know. He's the one was suspected all along, the one who got Gilman."

"Yes, except he denies it. He won't admit he was in the house at all. He denies killing Gilman, and there's no way we can prove it on him."

"Prove it on him?" Langdon was indignant. "You talk as though it was a crime or something. Prove it on him! There ought to be a reward."

"He don't need no reward. All he needs is he should get back where he was before all this happened. We know it was Gilman all along. We've got it proved with the adhesive tape it was Gilman all along, but people they aren't believing it. You can't tell them the kid he didn't have anything to do with it. Everybody's saying Herman was mixed up in it someway. You can't tell them he wasn't."

"People are crazy," Langdon said. "What can I do?"

"People they're saying Gilman is dead and that's great, but here's this other guy. He ain't dead. He was in it, too, and he's walking around loose. Nobody'll go near him. He can't get him no fights. He's as bad off as he ever was."

"I'm no rich man . . ." Langdon began.

Giordano waved his beginning away. "Not like that," he said. "That's not what I been thinking. Now if maybe you could go around and see him. You know, just to thank him like for what he done. He was too late to do you any good, I know, but still it's something to know Gilman was caught up with."

"Something?" Langdon groaned. "It's everything. It's all I've got."

"Yeah. You see, I tell him that what he done was great. It's nothing for him to be afraid of and nothing for him to be ashamed of. He had ought to be proud. He should want everybody to know. I tell him. The detectives—up to only the other day they was giving him a bad time— they tell him. But he don't trust us. Look, we're cops, and us cops we played every trick in the book on him trying to make him say he done what he never done. Now that we want him to tell what he did do only so all these people who keep saying he was mixed up in it some way, they'll know what way and they'll start treating him like he was a human again, he can't trust us. He thinks we're out to work another trick on him. Now you . . ."

"You think if I thank him, if I tell him what I think of him for what he did, if I tell him how I feel about him, it'll open him up?"

"Yeah, and if people see you, the two of you together. Having a drink like or something. It kind of would show them how it is. You know, you losing your wife and him losing his girl and both of them the same way. If it isn't too much to ask, Mr. Langdon. If you can't do it, I don't know anybody who could."

"It's the least I could do for the boy. Where do I find him?"

It was a Sunday morning and with Grady's bar not yet open, Frankie knew where Bob Herman would be. Langdon

walked around there with him. Sullenly long-suffering, Bob
unlocked the door and let them in.

"This here's the lady's husband, kid," Frankie said. "Mr.
Langdon."

Langdon put out his hand. "I want to shake your hand,"
he began. "I want to thank you."

"Leave me alone," he snarled. "Ain't you never going to
leave me alone?"

Taking them by surprise, he charged out between them,
sending Langdon reeling and shouldering Giordano out of
his way. Frankie made a belated grab at him, but Bob
slipped free. Since he took time out to assure himself that
Langdon was unhurt, Frankie for the moment lost the boy.
Bob had taken off on the run.

Frankie worked at apologizing for him. He didn't need
to. Langdon was understanding.

"Okay, he's sore at me," Frankie said. "He's got a right
to be sore at me, but he has no call to be taking it out on
you."

"He's got a right to be sore at the whole world," Langdon
said.

Giordano couldn't leave it at that. Now he was carrying
an additional burden. There was still what he felt he had
to do for Bob Herman, but now there was Langdon as well.
That had been a bad moment with Bob, and Frankie was
the one who had dragged Langdon into it. He was going
to have to do what he could to make that up to the poor
man. He was going to have to talk Bob into apologizing
or something. It was only decent.

He went looking for Bob. He had all manner of good
ideas on where to look. What of his own observation he
didn't know about the way Bob filled his days, he'd
been told by the precinct detectives. They knew from
those times when they had been "keeping an eye" on Herman. Frankie caught up with Bob in the park.

He had to work at it before Bob would talk to him at all. Then he had to work at it a lot more before Bob would tell him why he'd behaved that way with Langdon.

"You know why," Bob kept insisting.

"You're sore at me, but why at him?"

"You fucking well know why at him. You treat me like I was some shithead, like I was stupid maybe."

"He said you've got the right to be sore at the whole world," Frankie told him. "Maybe yes and maybe no, but it's no good, kid. Not the whole world. It's all the world you got."

"He knows damn well what right I got to be sore," Bob mumbled.

Frankie talked to him and Frankie sweated. At long last he had Bob talking and then Frankie listened. It was only after he'd heard everything that Bob had to say that he even began working on Bob to make the kid do what Frankie wanted of him. He'd begun on this only with the feeling that he would be happier if he could get Bob to go with him to Langdon and make his apologies. After hearing Bob out, he knew that it was mandatory that Bob do it. It wasn't easy, but eventually he did talk Bob into it. They went to the apartment together.

XVIII

It was a painful session. Wonderboy Herman sat looking down at his hands. He began well enough when Giordano introduced them all over again.

"Mr. Langdon," he gulped. "You her husband?"

"Yes, my boy. I'm her husband."

"Gee, I'm sorry. I know how you're feeling. Claire, now. We wasn't married or like that, but I know how you're feeling. I'm sorry."

"Thanks. I wish it could have been before . . ." Langdon faltered but, pulling together, he went on with it. "I wish it could have been in time to save my Harriet, but I'm glad you got him. I'm not a rich man, but any time, whatever it is, if there's anything I can do for you."

"For me? Why for me? It wasn't me, mister. It wasn't me got him. I wish it was. I'd have liked to, believe me, but it wasn't me."

"Look. We all know it was you. You were hanging around the place all the time. I saw you myself often enough."

"On the street outside the house. Never inside, mister. It wasn't me."

"But who else, my boy? Who else? If it was anyone else, they'd call the police and tell them the whole thing. Anyone else, they'd be looking for a reward, and if there was ever a time there should be a reward . . ."

"Mister, if it was me, I'd be going up and down the street telling everybody I done it and not for no reward neither. I'd be so happy, I'd be busting with it. I couldn't keep it to myself."

Langdon shook his head at him. "After what you've been through?" he said. "It was only because of you they found that Mrs. Burns's body, and did anybody thank you for it? They arrested you. They've been giving you a hard time ever since. I can understand you wouldn't see how this is different, but it is different, boy, believe me."

"It's no different. People is always telling me what I done when I ain't done it, like they know about me better than me. So what's different?"

Langdon tried to argue with him. "Gilman's different," he said. "Gilman's dead. He isn't around any more to tell those lies he kept telling, trying to frame you. Gilman's dead and it wasn't until he was dead that anybody could get any truth out of him. He never spoke a word of truth in his life, but his dead body told it for him. His dead body told all the truth anyone needs. Don't you even read the papers? They found the tape on him, the tape from the same roll he used when he went into the apartment at night and caught those poor women alone. That's the difference. We know who killed my wife and your girl and that first poor woman and the poor soul over in Brooklyn. That was all Gilman, and now he'll never be trying to put any of his doings on to you again. You ought to be proud."

"I had ought to've killed him that first time I tangled with him," the boy conceded. "I ain't got nothing to be proud of," he added. "I had nothing to do with it, not with none of it."

Shrugging in defeat, Langdon turned away from him. Giordano stepped into it.

"Mr. Langdon isn't completely right about this. They did find the tape on Gilman. Gilman was our man. He used his duplicate key to come into the apartment and kill

Emily Wilson. After the Wilson killing he had duplicate keys for both the locks and he used them and killed Claire Burns. The first time after he was through he cleaned up after himself and put on the second lock. The second time he changed the lock. Putting on the second lock and then changing it, he used that to cover himself. All this lock business kept saying it wasn't Gilman. It said it didn't happen any of the nights when he could have used his duplicate keys to get at these women. It happened only when there was a lock his keys wouldn't fit, a new lock with someone else holding the duplicate. When he killed Claire Burns, he made the bigger try at covering himself. He made the stab at putting it on you."

"And that poor Rose Eaton over in Brooklyn," Langdon put in. "He went there because we'd put a bolt on our door. He hadn't figured out yet how he would get past that bolt, so he had to go somewhere else. He tried it with a poor, old, drunken woman in the street, and it wasn't the same as creeping in on a woman and overpowering her before she was even awake. That old woman in Brooklyn gave him a fight. She broke his rib for him, so that wasn't any good. He went upstairs again and talked his way in."

"And Mrs. Langdon didn't put up any fight," Giordano murmured.

Langdon caught it and he flushed angrily. "Harriet was gentle. She was no fighter. She trusted him. He wasn't a stranger in the street. He had her overpowered before she even had the first idea of what he was after."

"Yeah," Giordano said. "That's what happened to her, but this one time it wasn't Gilman."

Bob Herman's head came up. His eyes came away from their study of his hands. He was bracing himself for the springing of the trap.

"That what you meant about me being wrong about the tape?" Langdon asked eagerly. "The tape he put on Harriet's lips wasn't from that same roll he'd been using. It said in the papers he had his whole damn chest taped up with stuff from that roll. He'd used the last of it. He had none left."

"Probably. But we haven't found any more tape that matches up with the piece used on your wife's lips. The tape tells us Gilman did the first three. It tells us nothing about Mrs. Langdon."

"It tells you he was the mad dog who was doing this horrible thing. He did it three times. You're going to say he didn't do it the fourth."

"The evidence says he didn't touch Mrs. Langdon."

"Ridiculous. No sensible man . . ." he began.

"No sensible man," Giordano interrupted him to say, "can believe he could change the lock on your door working without tools, and no sensible man can believe a corpse took his tools downstairs and put them away and then came back upstairs to lay down dead."

For a moment while he was taking it in, Langdon blinked stupidly. Then he whipped around, turning on Bob Herman. "You," he snarled. "That's why you're so modest. You weren't taking the credit for killing him. You weren't because you couldn't. You were the same as he was, and you went up there and did an imitation of what he'd been doing. You had to steal his key to get in there." He turned to Giordano. "That's it," he said in great excitement. "That's how it happened. Gilman missed the key. He went up to the apartment to check. He caught this man up there. That's how he got killed. This man had just changed the lock. He had the old lock still in his hand and he hit Gilman with it. Of course, there were no tools. They were this one's tools, and he took them away with him."

"Maybe you've got something there," Giordano purred. "The night old Rose Eaton was killed over in Brooklyn this boy couldn't get over there because all through the critical hours that night he was under surveillance. The night your wife was killed, Mr. Langdon, was different. Bob, here, wasn't under surveillance at all then because the man who tailed him the week before was too busy with other things the night Mrs. Langdon died."

Langdon turned on Frankie, rigid with quick hostility. "You people are to blame, too, then," he said. "If you're watching a man, what's the good of watching him one night and not every night?"

"We weren't watching him any night, Mr. Langdon," Giordano said. "The night he was watched, you was doing the watching. You moved your wife in here. You did everything you could to put her into the killer's hands, but he disappointed you. He didn't come. Even when Mrs. Langdon sat in here with the door open, waiting for him, he didn't come."

"I told you. Nobody can blame me more than I blame myself. And it's crazy saying it was me watching him that night. I wasn't even in the city. I was out of town on business."

"You were making it look like you was out of town on business. You were going to do it that night, Mr. Langdon, but you couldn't get near the house with Bob walking up and down in front of it. You had to wait till Bob was out of the way. You tailed him and you watched him. That's why he flipped when I took you around to see him and told him who you was. He thought I was lying to him, and he flipped. He thought he knew who you was. He thought you was a detective I figured he wouldn't spot, but he had you spotted from that night you tailed him. When he told me that, it changed everything. If one night when you was out of town you could still be around here tailing Bob, so why not this other night? You were going to do it that first night, but after you seen Bob go home to Grady's that night and you came back here after, you found the door was on the bolt. You had to go away and come back to try again after you made sure the door was never going to be bolted any more."

"Me?" Langdon yelped. "It was Gilman tried to get in that night. The door was bolted and he couldn't. That's why he went to Brooklyn."

"He went to Brooklyn because he thought you were out of town. He was afraid of what he'd do if he didn't get away from the house, and the way you was practically handing her to him had him scared. Some way he knew there was something wrong with you, Langdon. He would think you were out to trap him. How could he guess you were out to kill your wife?"

"Me?" Langdon moaned. "Since when does a man rape his own wife?"

"You was the one could get to her without stealing Gilman's key. You found a chance to slip into the house when Bob, here, wasn't around. You surprised the little woman by coming home when you was supposed to be out of town. That wouldn't scare her, would it? It was cozy. Going to bed with you, her dear husband, wouldn't scare her either. Of course, she didn't know what was happening to her. How could she? Gilman faked it with the lock changes. You faked a lot more of it. Taping her mouth, for instance. Gilman surprised them with the tape. He slapped it down over their mouths hard and quick and they tore their lips trying to get them unstuck so their screams could come through. When the tape was put on Mrs. Langdon's mouth, it was put on gentle, none of Gilman's roughness there. Also your wife didn't tear her lips. She never strained against the tape. She never tried to scream."

Langdon laughed. "You say there was nothing to frighten her about going to bed with me. I should hope not, for God's sake. You also say there was nothing to frighten her about me taping her mouth up? Why would she hold still for me doing that?"

"Because she was already dead when you put the tape on her. You killed her first and then you sealed her lips. It was only to make your killing look like the earlier ones."

Langdon forced a smile. "Now, look," he said, "you can't mean any of this. I was out of the city. You can check where I was that night."

"And we'll find one of them motels where a guest in an outlying cabin can check in of an evening and check out in the morning and leave his car parked there all night and nobody knows whether in between he's been off on a bus and back again or not."

"You must take me for a fool," Langdon said. "Say I did it. Say the whole thing went the way you're trying to make it. You know what I'd have done after I killed Gilman?"

"We know what you did do."

"I would have picked up the phone and called the police. I would have told them I came back to town unexpectedly and I surprised Gilman leaving my apartment. That I saw the lock lying on the floor near the door and I guessed what happened. I would have told them that I killed Gilman and would they please come and take the lousy, crazy, son-of-a-bitch's filthy, rotten body away because I wanted to be alone with my poor wife because she was lying dead on our bed where he abused her and killed her like he had those other women."

"Right," Frankie said. "You sure had you the murder that couldn't go wrong. You had it either way; if Gilman hadn't come along before you were away from the house, or if you could have known it was Gilman was the man we'd been looking for and that he had all that tape wrapped around him to prove it. You had no way of know-

ing that. The way you saw it, it would be your word only
to back up your story. You're no fool, mister. You weren't
kidding yourself that your bare word would be good
enough, not when you'd been working so carefully to set
your wife up for murder and not when calling the police
would have meant running out on a prepared alibi and
having to explain what your car was doing out of town
parked by a motel cabin you weren't using while you was
in town just missing out on saving your wife from Gilman.
You had to go back to the motel, mister, because you'd
have no way of explaining the motel setup. You were smart
enough to see you couldn't change your plan in midstream.
You were out of town. The unknown locksmith struck
again. You would mourn your wife even though she'd been
such an idiot that she'd let some smooth-talking rapist
talk her into repeating on the lock deal."

Langdon drew himself up. The outraged citizen putting
an erring public servant in his place, he glowered at
Frankie.

"Get out of here," he ordered. "I've had all of this I'm
going to take. Now you're getting out of here."

"Yeah," Frankie purred, "and I'm taking you with me.
If you had only known that Gilman had all the rest of the
tape he'd been using stuck right on to him, if you had only
known that the guy like labeled himself, you could have
set the thing up better. You wouldn't have gone to kill
yourself with any phony alibi."

"What do you mean," Langdon exploded, " 'if I had
only known.' When he came tiptoeing up to the door and
put his key in the lock and tried to work it and it wouldn't
work, and I was watching him through the peephole
and . . ."

He stopped short. The words had poured out of him
and he was too far into them before he recognized the
implications of what he was saying. His suppressed panic

exploded into the open as he did catch up with the meaning of what he'd let slip. He threw a frantic look toward the door but they were standing right over him, Frankie Giordano and Bob Herman. H. Conover (Just Call Me Con) Langdon wasn't going anywhere. He'd been.